TAKING THE CURE

Taking the Cure

A Novel

Sarah R Taggart

iUniverse, Inc.
New York Lincoln Shanghai

Taking the Cure
A Novel

iUniverse books may be ordered through booksellers or by contacting:

iUniverse
2021 Pine Lake Road, Suite 100
Lincoln, NE 68512
www.iuniverse.com
1-800-Authors (1-800-288-4677)

ISBN-13: 978-0-595-37890-6 (pbk)
ISBN-13: 978-0-595-82261-4 (ebk)
ISBN-10: 0-595-37890-0 (pbk)
ISBN-10: 0-595-82261-4 (ebk)

Printed in the United States of America

CHAPTER 1

▼

BAD TIMES

It's funny how you don't think about bad times. Wonderful really. The years go by, and you do what you have to do, and it begins to feel like it happened to someone else. Except at night you have dreams. Old men tell me they sometimes dream about the war—World War Two they mean. But mostly they don't talk about that and mostly I don't talk about my experience either.

At the time I didn't know what was coming. That was what was so scary. After all, you couldn't say to a fourteen year old, "Sorry but you are going to be flat in bed for four years, and we have this and this and this kinds of torture dreamed up to make your life miserable."

Instead I thought, Well I can stand anything for a month. Then, after I got to know a few people who had been around for a while, I let myself realize it might be several months. Then the disappointments started to pile up and it was a year. Then they started my pneumo and it was two years. Then my mother cut her visits down to once a month, and I got pretty upset because it was clear she wasn't expecting me home for a while.

I had been really tired all the time, and my mother decided I looked bad. Nothing you could put your finger on, but I was taking naps after school a lot. So when she told the doctor, he decided I should have a chest X-ray. It was 1944 and there were still lots of things around that could make you sick—polio and pneumonia and bad blood diseases. But I had never known about TB. Well, I had heard of it. Tuberculosis. But I never knew anyone who had it, and I certainly didn't know how they treated it.

I can't begin to tell you my mother's reaction when they finally told her. You'd think I'd done something wrong. She wouldn't believe it. "But we're not poor. We have good food. We don't know that kind of people." I couldn't figure out what she was talking about. She couldn't make herself say the word. Tuberculosis. She called it "Betsy's little problem." When Betsy's little problem got Betsy put in the hospital, she never gave it a name. She never told her friends, do you believe that? Made me feel like I was being punished for something and was being sent to jail.

Lucky for her the hospital was so far away so her friends weren't likely to come to see me. I didn't have a dad, and my brothers were both kids, so they weren't allowed to see me. Not my friends either; the visiting age was sixteen. So there I was, fourteen years old, locked up.

The state paid for it in those days. There was a law. Anyone with active TB was contagious and had to be in the hospital. If you didn't want to go, they could make you. You always had to wear a cloth mask over your nose and mouth when you were with other people, and so did they. It was like nobody had faces. Not that it mattered. My mother was my only visitor and she never got close enough to catch anything. At first she came twice a week, on Wednesdays and Sundays, and then on Sundays only. She could stay for an hour. That was all the visiting hours we had, one hour a day.

I had to be in bed one hundred percent of the time. People can't believe that. Like we had something wrong with our legs. The nurses and aides brought us bedpans and we weren't ever allowed to get up. We had to "take the cure." That's what it was called—"taking the cure." You had to lie flat on your back with just one skinny pillow; I don't know what two pillows would have done to us, made the blood rush to our legs maybe! Patients were allowed to roll over onto the side where their lesion was (TB was called a "lesion" when it was in your lungs) but they couldn't lie on the other side. That was because if they lay on top of their lesion it pushed it down and made it get better, but if they lay on the other side it would spread out. Really, that's what they told us. If you had lesions on both sides, like lots of people including me had, you just were supposed to stay on your back. And if you had trouble doing that, the nurses would give you a beanbag filled with buckshot for you to put on your chest to hold you down. Or, in my case, two shot bags.

I discovered there were lots of other unbelievable rules—at first I thought they were kidding. You were always supposed to keep your arms at your side, so that meant the girls couldn't set their hair. What's more, hair washing was supposed to tire you out, so you only got your hair washed every other week. Baths were supposed to make you tired too, so we got baths in bed twice a week. We sort of dabbed ourselves with washcloths in between times. And serious reading made you tired, so kids weren't allowed to continue their studies. Of course, knitting and sewing and any of that stuff could tire you, so they were against the rules.

Didn't leave a whole lot to do. We listened to the radio a lot; that was before TV of course. I once had a roommate with a record player—one of those fancy changers that dropped seventy eight inch records, one by one. You needed a crane to load the thing, but somehow that never got into the rule book and nobody noticed her putting five pounds of records at a time on that changer.

I started smoking in the hospital. That's something we were allowed to do. You could smoke lying flat on your back. Smoking and eating and drinking were very big. People's visitors would sneak in bottles and lots of visitors brought food. In fact, I was so skinny that everybody including the hospital tried to force food on me. People's relatives would bring me hamburgers and sandwiches just because they felt sorry for me. One time the dietician dreamed up a health drink that some of us had to take between meals four times a day. It looked like a milk-shake but it smelled like the inside of a barn and tasted terrible. They said it was filled with eggs and yeast and heavy cream. Anyway, it made me gag and they used to have to threaten me with "something worse" (there was always something worse they could do to you) to get me to take it. Finally somebody in the kitchen dipped a dirty finger into it and a whole batch got contaminated, so all of us who couldn't afford to lose weight got deathly sick and were hooked up to IV's and I'm just surprised nobody got sued. For sure they would these days. Would serve them right.

One thing that was surprising is that mostly people obeyed the rules. It shows you what fear of death will do. Once in a while someone would die, and the nurses would go up and down the hall closing the doors so they could get the person out without anybody seeing. A girl died right next door one time, and we could hear her begging for more blankets the night before she died. She was so cold; she kept saying it over and over, "I'm so cold!" That was enough to make you lie still, I'll tell you. We used to listen to her coughing too. It would wake us up.

Mostly the people I was with didn't cough. You had to be awfully sick before you coughed much, but we all had little cups beside our beds to collect sputum in case we did cough. I'm sorry, that's not very nice, is it? If you could spit up sputum you didn't have to have gastric aspirations. Once a month we shoved tubes down our noses into our stomachs and suctioned out gastric juices to be tested in the lab to see how contagious we were. For years I was just a little bit contagious. Then I would have a month when the culture was okay and then the bugs would appear again.

I always pictured them as little beetles with hard shells working away in my lungs. That was because when I first got to the hospital someone gave me an educational book to read and it showed little bacilli with faces that said things like, "We're very tough. We can't be killed, we can only be walled off by your body's defenses which will build a network of calcium to keep us inactive. But any time that network breaks down, we are there waiting to get busy again." It was not an encouraging thought. It did make me willing to drink lots of milk, though.

Most of the time I had just one roommate. That was always easier because then you didn't have to worry about them unloading some drip on you just because you had an empty bed in the corner of your four-bed ward. There was a lot of shifting around and you never had any say about who you got stuck with, or at least not until you had been there a long, long time. After I had been there for three years or so, I knew some of the nurses awfully well, and they wouldn't move me without making sure I didn't mind. Even in a place like that people eventually begin to feel bad for you.

The trouble was, my lesions kept breaking down. I would be stable for a while, and then pop, something would change. After the first year they started a pneumo-thorax in my right lung where the worst lesion was. They stuck a long needle between my ribs and injected air into the chest cavity outside the lung. That compressed the lung around the lesion and kept it from pumping in and out which supposedly broke down the calcium network. Twice a week I got a refill, because the air would be absorbed and the lung would start to expand again. It sounds worse than it was. The only thing I really minded was when I was a guinea pig for interns who couldn't find the way between the ribs—I didn't appreciate having my ribs used for target practice.

I don't even like to think about the broncoscopies. In order to make sure all that messing around wasn't causing problems that didn't show up on X-rays, I was regularly given broncs. Once again the residents and interns practiced on me, and sometimes they were good at getting that big pipe into my bronchial tubes and sometimes they weren't. When they weren't, I couldn't talk for days. So that was something to look forward to every few months. Naturally you took potluck with whoever was around to do it.

In my third year, I got moved into a double room with Polly Jo Williams. Polly Jo was my age, which was nice, and she had a terrific family. Her Mom used to buy me bed-jackets and she never came to visit without bringing me food; she was determined to "put some meat on your bones." Polly Jo had a brother in the army stationed in Germany; it was a lot of fun getting his letters. Polly Jo had caught TB in nursing school. Lots of nursing and medical students caught it, so her family wasn't strange about it the way my family was. In fact, she was so matter of fact it really was a help to me. She had loads of friends who worked in the hospital who could sneak in to see her at odd hours, and she wasn't scared. That was the big thing. She knew about TB and she wasn't scared. "If I don't get better here, I'll say forget it and go home." But things tended to work out for Polly Jo, so I don't think she ever seriously thought she wouldn't get better.

She was so cute. Whereas I was a bag of bones with plain straight blonde hair hanging down my back and a plain nothing kind of face (people said I had "lovely coloring" but that was just because I hadn't been outdoors in so long that I didn't have any freckles or spots.) Polly Jo had curly brown hair and a ragamuffin face, with dimples and bright blue eyes. I didn't know how big she was because I never saw her standing up, but she seemed to me to be little, looked at lying down. Actually she sat up a lot, which you weren't supposed to do, so I could sort of guess her size minus her legs. Her family was from the South, so she talked cute too; I loved to listen to them talk to each other. They called everybody "honey"" and "you-all" and everything was "ole," like "this-here ole place," and "that ole doctor," and stuff like that. Her dad had come north during the war to work in the bomber plant, and the money was so good they decided to stay. Polly Jo used to tell me about living in the South when she was a little girl. It sounded wonderful.

I guess when the hospital was built in 1925 or so it was the fanciest building the town. But when I was there it was just big and old and mean looking. It had underground passageways and windows that were deliberately made to be hard to get out of. I remember once someone jumped off a tenth floor porch railing and went right by our window; until then I'd never stopped to think that might be something a person would want to do. The hospital had a nice location though, on a hilltop facing away from the river valley. In the fall the valley is so beautiful; sometimes when we were being wheeled on stretchers to physical exams or to get our hair washed, or to pneumos, they would stop and let us look out the back windows at the trees. Our rooms all faced the front so mostly we looked at the tops of visitors' cars.

I had always heard that the county san (real TB hospitals were called sanitoriums), about thirty miles north of us, looked like a private club out in the country with beautiful lawns and gardens. Still, we thought people who went there didn't get well; there were lots of stories about how many breakdowns you could expect if you took your cure at the san. I guess that rumor was the hospital's way of bullying us into staying where we were. We were part of a scientific experiment and if we caught onto the idea that at the san you got to walk around, go home on weekend passes and have boy friends, we weren't likely to settle for being in bed all the time with no vacations.

There were usually about twenty patients on our floor and after a while we knew all of them because when we were already on stretchers ("gurneys") going for X-rays or treatments, we could ask to be wheeled into other rooms for visits. Our favorite person to visit was a bachelor college professor named Mr. Adams. He was an old guy and I heard later that he was a famous person, but we liked him because he knew so many dirty jokes. He loved to tell us about the wicked world and try to shock us. "Just you wait," he would say. "You girls are in for a lot of surprises." There were really terrible rumors around about him but I didn't believe any of them; I thought people were just jealous because he was smart and well-known. He was pessimistic about himself; he was sure it was "all over." Actually, he got out and was still going strong the last time I heard about him, so that just went to prove that you never could tell.

The people who were the most important to us were the nurses. The doctors could decide the big things, but our regular routine depended on the nurses and the aides. It's funny the things you remember. The good nurses were the ones who made really tight beds and gave nice firm bed baths; I couldn't stand to fight against a loose bottom sheet or to be wiped instead of scrubbed. In those days the nurses did everything: carried bedpans, delivered trays, pushed nourishment cars, the dirty jobs as well as the medical ones—very different from today.

Our head nurse was Miss Ebersole. She cared a lot about how things looked, so she would wander up and down the hall checking to see if the window shades were all rolled down the same distance and whether our night stands were neat. I was afraid of her. She never ever smiled and mainly we saw her when she would sail in front of the doctors during rounds. We had "small rounds" every morning and "grand rounds" every Saturday, when the chief of staff—he was always referred to as "the Chief"—and all the visiting docs would stand around and talk about us like we weren't there. Miss E. would take notes on a clip board while the doctors talked. I always wondered what she wrote down. She cozied up to the doctors so much it was disgusting, but she treated us patients like we had a contagious disease or something!

The best nurses and doctors were always the ones who had had TB themselves. There were usually two or three nurses who had taken the cure and they could joke around with us about it. Also our favorite doctor, Dave Burson, had caught TB while he was in medical school and he planned to make TB his career. Over the years I saw him graduate from being an intern in a short white coat to a resident in a long white coat—the day we first saw his long coat everybody up and down the hall applauded. We called him Dave—nobody ever used his last name. He loved to make excuses to sit in our room and just talk to us. We were a big club—long ago TB was known as consumption and we referred to ourselves as consumptives.

Dave had a wife and a couple of kids, but one day Professor Adams let a nasty remark drop about him. "He's spending a lot of time in the treatment room with Sue Ellen," he told us. I thought he was just telling stories as usual, but then I started seeing them walking with their arms around each other. Sue Ellen was our favorite nurse. She looked like Betty Grable, the movie star, but she was nice too and she would sometimes help me with my hair—she cut it for me, and once she even sneaked me an extra shampoo. I used to ask her about her boy friends and I tried to imagine what it would be like to be her. So I knew that she and Dave were good friends and weren't really doing anything wrong and I thought the professor had a dirty mind. I told him so, too. He just laughed at me.

I thought that Polly Jo agreed with me, but she kept her mouth shut about it. Then one day Sue Ellen was gone. Nobody would tell us where she was. We didn't see Dave either for a while. Then he'd sulk around with a cross look on his face and wouldn't talk to us. We didn't find out till a long time later what had happened.

CHAPTER 2

▼

THE ESCAPE

One day, somewhere at the end of my fourth year, a whole crowd of doctors came in to see me after staff meeting. That was always a bad sign. One doctor at a time didn't ever worry me too much, but when they came in bunches it usually meant trouble. Dave was the resident at that point and he sat down beside my bed. The rest of them stood at the end and watched.

"Betsy, we've decided to let your pneumo out."

Even though that meant they wouldn't be sticking needles in my ribs any more, I was suspicious. It sounded like good news, but why the big production?

"You know that you've got adhesions and four years is a long time to carry a pneumo. We just don't think it is a good idea to continue it," Dave said.

I didn't comment. Dave frowned because he could see the smooth talk wasn't helping.

"Okay," he said, "you probably know what we're thinking about."

I took a deep breath while I considered what he was saying, and then I panicked. "A thoracoplasty?" I could hardly say the word. I prayed he would shake his head.

"A thoracoplasty."

I had never cried in front of that many doctors, but I couldn't help it. I rolled over on my good side with my back to Dave and closed my eyes. The tears leaked out on the pillow, but I didn't say a word. I heard Polly Jo say something.

"Leave her alone Dave. She'll be okay."

Dave stood up. "I'll be back later, Betsy. We can talk about it then." They left and closed the door behind them.

I started to scream "no!" as loud as I could when I felt a firm hand clamped over my mouth. Polly Jo had jumped out of bed and was sitting on my bed keeping me from screaming. I had never seen her out of bed before. I was so shocked it calmed me down.

"Polly Jo, they'll see you. Get back in bed."

"Bonesy, you mustn't yell. We'll think of something, honey, but you mustn't yell." She let up on my shoulder, which she had been squeezing real hard, and when she saw that I was under control she went back and climbed onto her bed. She sat bolt up, her legs crossed and her fists clenched. I could see that she was crying too. "They can't do that to you," she said. "You mustn't let them do that to you."

I sat up and rolled my thin little pillow into a prop. I leaned back against the metal headboard of my bed. It felt cold and hard. I thumped my head against it a couple of times and tried to get my heart to slow down. A thoracoplasty was the ultimate torture. They took out enough of your ribs to permanently collapse part of your chest. As if that wasn't bad enough, it usually took more than one operation, and it was, of course, permanent. I had seen them and they didn't look nice.

"Oh boy," was all I could manage to say. My mouth was dry. I had been scared lots of times before, but those were nothing compared to this. All I could think of was, I'm too young for a thoracoplasty, I'd rather be dead.

"Polly Jo," I finally said, "I'm never going to get out of here. I'm going to be here the rest of my life."

"Betsy-Bones, what are you talking about? He didn't say anything about how long you're gonna to have to stay. He just said they were gonna to let your pneumo out."

"Suppose a thoracoplasty doesn't work? Then what?"

"Well honey, I guess you cross that bridge when you get to it. You gotta have some good luck some time." But I didn't think her voice had much conviction to it. "What're you gonna do, honey? You don't have much choice do you?"

"I could say no."

"You gonna say no to that big bunch of white coats?"

My head started to pound and I felt numb. I couldn't think. "I've got to get out of here." It was an insistent sentence I kept hearing in my mind. "I've got to get out of here, Polly Jo."

"We all feel that way sometimes, Bonesy."

"No, I mean it. I've been here for nearly five years. I'm going to die here if I don't get out."

"Nobody's going to die."

"Yes, I am. Why else do they keep me in bed? Why do they keep trying new things on me? Do you know that I've been here longer than anybody except Marcella?" Marcella had TB of the spine and was on a Stryker Frame. She had been there for nine years.

"I don't know, Betsy. You haven't had any of the breaks, that's for sure true."

"I feel like walking out right now."

"Like that? In your nightgown?"

"I'll sneak out in the middle of the night. They'll find me frozen stiff down by the river. It'll serve them right." That was a slightly funny thought and I relaxed a little. Still, it didn't make the thoracoplasty go away.

I thought about it. "I wonder how long it'll take to let the pneumo out."

Polly Jo put on her nursing hat. "Seems to me it takes a month or so. Maybe two months. They can't do it all at once."

"So they can't do anything else to me for at least a month."

"Honey, they can always do something else to you. But I don't suppose they can start skinning your ribs for at least a month."

"Then I have at least a month to plan how to get out of here."

"Bonesy! What is the matter with you? You can say 'no', but you can't leave! Honey, that's crazy."

Suddenly I was just as calm as calm can be. It was just as clear as a bell. I was going to leave. I had a month to figure out how to do it. If it killed me, well staying might kill me too. At least I'd have a little while of real life. I looked over at Polly Jo. Would she help me or would she tell on me? I thought about it for a few minutes.

Polly Jo studied me. "Bonesy, what in the world are you thinkin' about? You look like you're gonna to bend nails. You're worryin' me, honey."

I realized I had no choice. I couldn't possibly do it without her help. "Polly Jo, please don't say anything or give me an answer till you've thought about it for a long time. And please don't say anything to anyone. Promise me."

"Promise you what?"

"I'm not crazy. Really I'm not. But I've been in this place since I was fourteen years old and I don't want a thoracoplasty. I'm only eighteen. I've never had a boy friend, never been on a date, never done anything. Who'll want me with a caved-in chest? I don't know what I'm going to do, but whatever I do, I'll have to have your help. So please, promise you'll help me no matter what."

Polly Jo had tears in her eyes again. She shook her head like her brains were rattling, then she shrugged. "Well," she finally said with a sigh, "you may be crazy but I can understand how you feel." She was quiet for a minute, staring at me. "Okay," she said hesitantly, "this may be an awful mistake, but if you're positive that's what you have to do then I guess you have to do it. And I sure as the world wouldn't ever tell anybody, you can count on that." She looked away and gently made me a promise. "I'll help you no matter what."

So it was settled.

*   *   *   *

When we first began to think about it we could see a whole lot of problems. The main one we thought about was money.

"How much do you think I'll need?" I asked Polly Jo. I hadn't ever used money except to buy candy and cigarettes. I didn't even know how much anything cost.

Polly Jo loved figuring things out. "Let's see. If you find you a room in a boarding house and buy lots of milk and peanut butter, I'll bet you can get by with two hundred dollars to start."

"To start?"

"Well honey, you're gonna to have to get a job."

So that brought up another problem. I didn't know if I could walk from my bed to the door. How was I ever going to have strength enough to have a job.

"That's what we're going to use this month for." said Polly Jo. "To get you in shape."

Get me in shape. That was a good one. Kill me more likely.

"Bones, do you want to leave here or not? You can't exactly order yourself a wheelchair you know." Polly Jo had gotten into the spirit of the big escape plot and now she was the one who was do or die. Well why not—it wasn't her life! Sometimes her enthusiasm scared me a little. Later on I would appreciate it plenty, but even though it had been my idea, when we first started planning I'll admit to some cold feet.

"Just think about the alternatives, honey," Polly Jo would say, and that would usually firm me up some.

We began right away to get me out of bed. We would wait until everybody's doors were closed at 9:30 at night, and then we started on what Polly Jo called my "training program." I'll never forget the first night I got up. I was so dizzy I thought I would keel over, and my legs felt like they belonged to someone else.

The floor looked a mile away. I just fell into the chair by my bed and started to cry.

"This is never going to work."

"Well, for heaven sakes, Betsy, what did you expect?" Polly Jo was all fired up. "You've been in that ole bed for nearly five years. I'm surprised you remember how to do it."

But the second night it was a little easier and the third night I kicked the chair away from the bed so I had to take a couple of steps. I would sit in the chair for half an hour or so, praying that the junior night nurse wouldn't burst in on us, and then I would practice standing until I started to get dizzy.

After two weeks, I could walk the length of the room fairly steadily, and we started the "hiking" phase of the training program. Every night I walked from the door to the window and back, until finally I could keep walking for ten or fifteen minutes without feeling faint. Polly Jo couldn't stand it to watch me from her bed, so she would get up and sit in a chair to cheer me on.

The money part of it was harder. I never had more than the ten dollars at a time that my mother would mail to me—by then she never visited—and Polly Jo's savings money was in the bank. Finally we decided we had to have another accomplice. We decided on a girl named Nancy who was ward clerk on one of the surgery floors. She and Polly Jo had gone to high school together and she just hated the hospital. She used to say over and over that she didn't see how we could stand it and she used to come visit at all kinds of off-hours, so we knew she didn't care about rules. "She'll think it's exciting," was Polly Jo's guess.

Nancy was perfect. Like Polly Jo said, she was a born spy, and once we had someone helping us in the outside world everything was a whole lot easier. She went to the bank and got out Polly Jo's savings, which came to a hundred and thirty five dollars, and then she put in fifty dollars of her own. I couldn't believe it. "I'll pay you back just as soon as I can," I kept assuring them, but they said it was okay, not to worry about it. With the money I managed to save (I bummed a lot of cigarettes) I had my two hundred dollars.

The other big problem that stumped us at first was that I didn't have any street clothes. Polly Jo's clothes would be too small and so would mine; I had grown some since I was fourteen. I wasn't even sure what size I wore. But once again, Nancy came through for us. She took a flyer on a size ten dress—I was thin even though I was tall—and size eight shoes, and smuggled them in during one of her visits. We told the nurses they belonged to a visitor who had left them by mistake. Since they were in a flat department store box, it wasn't too unlikely a story. And amazingly enough, they fit. Well, the skirt of the dress was a little short—those were days when skirts were practically to your ankles—but that was minor. The shoes felt so funny. They were high-heeled sandals and I had to practice walking in them, which was really hard to do. Since it was summer I didn't have to worry about a coat, but Nancy said she had a coat she would give me as soon as I got out. It wasn't till later that I started worrying about things like being cold.

My next X-ray was due the first week in September and we knew that after that I would be up for another staffing. I was down to one pneumo every ten days, so about the middle of August we picked a date. August 25th. Sunday. Nancy was off work that weekend and could find a room for me. We decided it would be a good idea if Polly Jo didn't know where I was; that way she couldn't possibly let it slip.

"What are you so nervous about?" Nancy asked me once.

I explained that it was against the law to be out of the hospital.

"Well, suppose they find you. What worse can they do to you than bring you back here?"

"That's bad enough," I agreed, "but what I really think they would do would be to lock me up."

"Lock you up? How could they do that?"

"There's a TB ward at the state mental hospital. Once I run away from here, they're going to think I've cracked up." It was true. I had never known anybody who did what I was planning to do, but I had known people to go on hunger strikes or to quit sleeping or to start yelling, and they always packed them off to the mental hospital. Or at least, those were the rumors.

I had been afraid of so many things for so long that my nervousness felt familiar when the big day started to get closer. I was famous on the floor for my fast pulse and you better believe it didn't slow down any. And I developed funny little superstitions. Like if it's hot that week, that'll be a good sign, or if old deaf Maggie Dillard is the night nurse that week I'll get away with it, or if I get a cold it'll mean I'm not supposed to do it. I didn't tell Polly Jo about those ideas though. I don't think she believed in silly stuff like that.

Sure enough the 25th was hot all day. I gagged on my lunch and choked down enough dinner to get by. I'll bet I looked at my bed-stand clock fifty times. I could hardly believe time was passing at all. PJ got grim and silent, so she wasn't any help, but when I asked what was wrong she pretended to smile and said she knew everything was going to be fine, even though I could see now she had her doubts. It's a little late for that, I thought. This was no time to chicken out.

I planned to leave during the shift change at eleven that night. The junior night nurse was new, a lucky break, so I figured she wouldn't know if the sounds from the hall seemed funny. And sure enough Mrs. Dillard was going to be on senior night—I had asked about that when an aide brought my dinner tray. I knew everybody gathered in the nurses' station to look at charts when the late night shift came on duty, after the intern had made his evening rounds. I thought I could get from our room to the stairwell without anybody seeing me.

That's just how it worked out. I waited till I could hear three voices all in one place through a crack in the door, and then I hugged Polly Jo, took my things that were stuffed in the department store box: my nighties and stuff from my night stand and a couple of bed jackets. Then I slid through the barely opened door. When I noticed that my new shoes were going to click-clack I bent over and quick took them off, holding my breath that nobody had heard. Then I walked real fast in the other direction from the nurses' station toward the red exit sign. Nancy was supposed to meet me at the employee's entrance with a car, so all I had to do now was walk was down three flights of stairs.

When you think about something over and over the way I had, you think you know just what it will be like. I thought I would be scared. But once I made it to the stairwell, I felt like it was all over. I was safe. And I felt so elated. From there on everything was new. I hadn't been able to imagine it. The stairwell was cold and breezy and the damp concrete sort of stuck to my stocking feet as I hurried down the steps. My knees didn't feel very secure—I never had stopped to think about stairs being different from just walking—but I paid attention to where I put my feet and pretty soon I was at the bottom.

When I pushed through that heavy door to the outside I thought I was in heaven. The night was so big I couldn't believe it. I could hear faint sounds that weren't echoey the way they are inside, and when I looked up there wasn't any ceiling, just stars going as far away in every direction as I could look. The air smelled so light and clean that I thought, "If I can just stand here forever I'll be happy." As long as I live, that experience of going outdoors after four years inside will be the best few minutes I ever had.

I heard Nancy's voice saying, "Betsy, I'm over here." Her voice sounded so soft and quiet—I never knew before that voices outside were different; I'll bet most people never notice. There's such a long long way for the sound waves to go I guess. Nancy was standing beside an old blue Ford sedan. I walked over to her and said, "Hi." Then I laughed; my voice sounded real funny too. Quiet and far away. Nancy didn't know what I was laughing at of course, so she asked me if I was okay and then took my box and put it in the back seat. Then she pointed at my feet and I remembered about the shoes I was still carrying. While she went around to her side of the car I sat sideways on the seat and put my shoes back on. Then I sat around straight and shut my car door. I was still excited and not scared.

"Where are we going?" I asked as Nancy started the engine.

"Not too far, I'm sorry to say," Nancy said. "The only room I could find that you can afford is in a tourist home around the corner."

My heart sank. Around the corner? Where people I knew would be walking by every day?

"Well look, Betsy. I thought about it. You aren't going to want to go out much for a few weeks, and I thought up a perfect excuse for your landlady. I told her you had a blood disease, not contagious, but that you had to be near the hospital for treatments. I said you got tired real easily and that you would be spending a lot of time in your room. She never even questioned me. She said she had had lots of roomers like that. I told her how nice you are and that you didn't know exactly how long you would be staying. Also, it's close, so I can bring you food and keep an eye on you."

Suddenly a thought occurred to me. "How are you going to explain my coming at this hour? And not having a suitcase?"

Nancy glanced over at me and grinned. "You do have a suitcase. It's in the trunk. And what's more, it's packed for you."

Nancy had found me a suitcase and some new clothes? I was overwhelmed.

"Oh Nancy! I couldn't have done this without you," I said. "How'll I ever repay you?"

It suddenly felt like too much. My calmness was beginning to dissolve into tears. I bit my lip and took a deep breath to settle the feelings down.

Nancy was tough and determined even though she was sort of scolding me. "You behave yourself and get well," she said. "I just don't think anybody gets better in that hole."

It turned out that Nancy had told Mrs. Boyle, the landlady, that I was coming at 11:30 because I couldn't get a bus from my home town earlier than that. Nancy made up a town. She told her she was meeting me at the bus station. I hoped I could remember all those stories if Mrs. Boyle ever asked me about them.

The tourist home was an old house practically on the sidewalk, with grey asphalt siding. There was a sign hanging on the side of the house. "Rooms For Rent." We parked in the narrow driveway and Nancy pulled a big old brown suitcase out of the trunk. Mrs. Boyle was wearing a robe and bedroom slippers when she let us onto the glassed-in porch. She was a skinny older lady with a lined face and scraggly gray hair.

"So you're Jan," she said to me.

Jan? Nancy had made up a name for me. Jan Drew. The Drew part was of course from the Nancy Drew mysteries. Of all the stories that Nancy concocted, for a while that new name turned out to be the most important.

Nancy handed me the suitcase and waved goodnight; I was glad she wasn't a hugger. Mrs. Boyle took me into the house, up some narrow steep stairs, and down a dark hall to a small room at the end. She showed me that some extra stairs went down from my room to the kitchen—she said this was once a maid's room. She hoped I didn't mind. I was so tense and tired by then I wouldn't have minded anything but I tried to be polite. Then she took me next door where there was a little bathroom with a real shower—I hadn't had a real shower in all those years, but of course I didn't tell her that. She said that it being summer I was her only guest but because my friend had said money was a problem she was putting me in her cheapest room. She asked again if I minded, but of course I didn't.

After she left me I shut the door and put my suitcase on the table by the window. I sat down on the low bed. I noticed that the bed didn't have a headboard—I had never seen a bed that was just a mattress and springs with metal legs. The only other furniture was a straight chair that had a blue plastic seat and shiny metal legs, and an old wooden bureau, dark colored with drawers that didn't quite fit.

I was too tired and excited to try to go to sleep—my pulse was out of control and I felt jittery right down to my fingernails. So I decided to put stuff away in order to have something to do. I opened the suitcase and there on top was a tablet of writing paper, some envelopes and a pencil. Nancy had thought of everything. So sort of desperately I decided I should write my mom a letter, even though by that time I pretty much never saw her. Still I always hoped that she thought about me sometimes.

"Dear Mom, You will know by now that I left the hospital. I'm sorry to worry you but I can't let anyone know where I am because I don't want to be locked up again. I'm all right. (I underlined that a couple of times.)

From time to time I will write to you, but for now just please don't worry and I'm really sorry.

love,

Betsy."

Just writing that letter wore me out, and of course I didn't have any stamps so I didn't know how I would mail it, but I thought maybe Nancy wouldn't mind doing it. I hoped in a few days I could make it to the stores across the street that I could see through the window. But that night one letter was the limit of what I could manage.

Finally I went to bed and my mind just went dark—I must have fallen asleep almost as soon as my feet left the floor. At eight I woke up, stumbled next door to the toilet, and then went back to sleep again. I suppose it was about four in the afternoon when I was waked up by someone knocking on my door.

"Betsy? It's me." Nancy's voice was hushed.

It took me a minute to organize my woolly thoughts, but as reality crashed in I pulled myself up out of bed and let her in. My head was throbbing and my legs felt wobbly.

"I brought you a hamburger and a milk shake. Did I wake you up?"

I looked at the cardboard container cautiously. "Gosh, I don't know if I can eat anything." I was aware of feeling nauseated and I definitely had a headache.

"Well try the milk shake anyway. You've got to eat. How did you sleep? How do you feel?" She looked genuinely worried. I must have been a sight with my pale skin and bags under my eyes. I took a few sips of the milk shake and discovered to my surprise that it tasted good.

"I think I'm hungry," I said. "Maybe I'll feel better after I eat."

"Well you wouldn't believe the hoorah at the hospital," Nancy reported, after I had perked up a little. "I sneaked in to see Polly Jo after lunch and she said the police had been in to see her."

"The police?" I was alarmed. "What did she tell them? She didn't tell them about you, did she?"

"Naw. She said she just kept telling them that she didn't know where you were; that you had a friend on the outside who she didn't know and that you left in the middle of the night. She made out that you were having a romance!" Nancy laughed. "So they are trying to figure out what boys you might have known."

I breathed a sigh of relief. That really had been a big worry. I knew how fast talking some of those doctors can be and I could just picture a bunch of them taking Polly Jo into a conference room and explaining real seriously to her how my life and the lives of others were "in jeopardy." They would make it sound like not only was I going to give TB to the whole world, but didn't she understand that mentally I wasn't...well, you know. But police! My goodness, Polly Jo wouldn't have any trouble with the police. I bet they thought she was cute, but also, I bet they wanted to get out of there real fast so they wouldn't catch anything. I had seen outsiders like that who had to visit because it was their duty. They always stood with one hand on the doorknob!

*　　　*　　　*　　　*

Nancy had figured out that for a week or so I would need her to come in every day, and then maybe I could try walking across the street. At first just walking to the john was a chore, and also Nancy put milk and eggs and butter in Mrs. Boyle's refrigerator for me, so once a day at least I walked slowly down the back stairs to the kitchen. When Mrs. Boyle heard about the hot plate she said please would I use the kitchen stove because she was afraid of fire. But she was real nice about it, and even sometimes would give me food she was cooking.

"What's the matter with your blood, if you don't mind my asking?" she asked me one time.

"They think I have serum hemotome." I invented as obscure a combination of medical words as I could think of.

"Oh is that right? What are they doing for it?" She knew I never left the house, so that was a tricky question. I thought fast.

"Well, they can't do much yet, but they want me nearby in case the medicine gives me side effects." I was deliberately vague, hoping she would let it go.

"Oh I know," she said sympathetically. "I once had a man here who would get to trembling from head to foot from the medicine he took. Makes you wonder if it wouldn't be better to be sick."

When she asked about my family I did a terrible thing. I hinted it was a hereditary disease that they were embarrassed about and that's why they couldn't visit me. I think Mrs. Boyle had seen so many strange illnesses in all the years she had been running that rooming house that she would believe anything. She just clucked and said, "Too bad. That's really too bad."

*   *   *   *

One day, about two weeks later, when Nancy came, she brought a letter from Polly Jo. It said:

Dear Bonesy, I hope I don't get us both in trouble writing this, but I think about you all the time and I keep thinking of things I want to tell you. Don't answer this—I'm sure everybody is watching to see if I hear from you. We were right to ask N. to help us because I don't think anybody knows we are friends. Lately she has been coming in during rest hour when all the doors are closed. You'll have to ask her how she does it. She has a story to explain why she has to be on the floor, and then when no one is looking, in she comes. (If anybody else ever reads this letter, we are in trouble!)

People talk about you all the time. The police haven't been back, but periodically the Chief huffs and puffs in and gives me a little lecture, and Dave often comes in and sits and looks worried. Actually, he thinks I communicate with you (smart man) so he tells me things he thinks you ought to know. So this is from him; be sure to drink a quart of milk every single day, be sure to take cod liver oil pills, be sure to take a nap every day, if you think you have an afternoon temperature drop everything and go to bed, if you start having night sweats come back to the hospital. I think that last is right, honey. That would be a bad sign. Dave says he would want you to know that he understands why you did it, and they wouldn't have jammed a thoracoplasty down your throat if they'd known you were that scared. I wish I thought he was in charge, because I trust him, but I don't trust the Chief, so I guess you're on your own for a while. But Dave and I can play 'what if'—like what if Betsy needed some penicillin or something. Where could she go? I think he would tell me without telling me, if you know what I mean.

"They moved Marcella in with me. Do you believe that? What a dumb thing to do with the one other person in the whole world who would never tell. She thinks it's wonderful; she says to tell you she's jealous but she knows in her bones (ha, ha) that you're going to be fine. Do you know that I think that stupid head nurse thinks she's punishing me by giving me Marcella, but of course we get along fine, and I don't mind her frame a bit. As you know, she's a terrific good sport about it. As she says, she might as well be.

Well honey, I'll stop for now. My Mom and Dad send their love—no, I didn't tell them anything, but they're nobody's fool. My Mom says EAT.

love from us all,

P.J.

*   *   *   *

Around October, I started doing some little chores around the house for Mrs. Boyle. I would go out of the house during the day and pretend I had been to the hospital to get medicine. I would try to go on nice sunny days when I could walk to a park about four blocks away. Sitting in the sun was bliss, even thought I knew sunshine was supposed to be bad for you. One morning I looked in my mirror and I had a little bit of sunburn. I thought to myself, you look like a real person.

The chores helped out for the food I ate. Mrs. Boyle couldn't stand to see me eat all those eggs and all that peanut butter and I really think she like having somebody to cook for. When I said I couldn't pay, she said I could dust and keep the bathrooms clean. Later on I vacuumed some too. I liked doing it and my two hundred dollars lasted longer that way. But by the time the cold weather started, towards Halloween, I was getting awful low on money. Also, the coat Nancy gave me was a fall coat. I got to worrying what I would wear when it started to snow. But I couldn't get a part time job that I could do. I knew I couldn't stay on my feet enough to waitress and the cashier's jobs that were near were full time. I just really couldn't think what I could do that would be sitting down and also let me take naps. So when Mrs. Boyle let me do housework, I jumped at the chance.

Still, it didn't get me any cash, so when Nancy brought me a letter from my mother with money in it, I could have cried for joy. It turned out my mother wasn't a fool either. My brother had talked on the phone to Dave and he told him he was positive Polly Jo knew where I was. So my brother played "what if" too—if Polly Jo could get a letter to me, did she think I could use money. I don't know how Polly Jo managed to tell him how broke I was, but there was a check for $100 with the letter (that was a lot in those days) and my mother's letter said if I cashed the check she would know I needed it and she would send more. I figured I could pay my back rent, buy a warm coat for about $25 and still have money left for other winter clothes. Mrs. Boyle told me about a secondhand store where they have stuff really cheap and told me how to take a taxi there and back. That was the beginning of my troubles.

CHAPTER 3

▼

FAMILIES

Nancy's visits slacked off after a month or so when she saw I was making it okay. I used to talk to girls who were at the park with their babies, but I figured I shouldn't get too close because I didn't know how contagious I was. Other than Mrs. Boyle, I didn't have much of anybody to talk to. So one day near Thanksgiving you can imagine how surprised I was when Mrs. Boyle knocked on my door and told me there was a young man to see me. I didn't know if I should go down or not, or maybe run out the back door! but by then I felt pretty safe, so my curiosity got the best of me. I knew absolutely right away who he was. When I walked in the front room, a small wiry guy about five feet seven, with curly brown hair and a baby face stood up. He looked just like Polly Jo.

"Are you Bonesy?" he asked. "Hi, I'm Jimmy Williams." We shook hands.

I couldn't stop smiling, it was so funny to see the resemblance. "You look just exactly like your sister," I said several times.

"Seen one Williams, seen 'em all, I guess."

I told him to sit down and then I sat down across from him, and then it hit me.

"How did you know where I was? Polly Jo doesn't even know."

"I've known Nancy for a long long time," he said confidently, as though that explained it.

"I don't understand. Why did you want to come here?"

He looked thoughtful. "Well, after all those letters you wrote me in Germany, I felt as though we were friends. And when Polly Jo wrote and told me what you'd done, I thought you were one brave kid. So when I got home last week, I made up my mind to try to find you, to see if I could help you."

"Does Polly Jo know you're here?"

"Not yet. Did you know she's getting out pretty soon?"

"Oh my goodness." I was overwhelmed. "That's wonderful news. When?"

"Maybe right after New Years."

Jimmy asked me if I ever went out anywhere and would I like to go for a ride in his car. It happened so fast that I didn't have time to worry what I looked like or if it was a real date or anything.

I ran upstairs and got a coat and then hurried outside without saying anything to Mrs. Boyle. After we got in the car I felt awkward. I didn't know how to act with a boy. I sat very still and clasped my hands together and looked straight out the windshield.

Jimmy said, "Where'd you like to go?" and I tried to sound nonchalant.

"You decide," I said, sneaking a sidewise glance at him. He looked as if he always smiled; his face was dimply and I wondered if he was laughing at me. "Did I say something funny?" I asked him.

I felt even more uncomfortable when he looked right at me from so close. "You can relax," he said. "I'm just taking you for a little ride. It's okay, isn't it? It won't tire you out or anything?"

I smiled at him but I wasn't relaxed. "It's fine. I'm just not used to doing this."

"Right-o," he said loudly, and cranked on the motor. "Here we go." And we spun away from the curb with the tires squealing. I looked back at the house and saw Mrs. Boyle standing in the doorway, her eyes popping. Poor Mrs. Boyle, it wasn't very nice to go off like that without an explanation, after all she had done for me.

Jimmy tried to make conversation as we rode along. "How long are you going to stay in that rooming house?" I explained that I wasn't strong enough yet to get a job. "But are you better? How'll you know when you're well?"

That was the big question, of course. I hadn't let myself think much about it. I told him I thought I was better but I had no way to know for sure. I had gained weight, I didn't get tired so easily, and I thought I looked better in the mirror, though that could just be because I got outdoors some.

"Where's your mom? You have a family some place don't you?"

I was surprised we hadn't talked about that in our letters; it seemed to me we talked about most everything else. "My Mom is at home with my little brothers. I guess they're not so little anymore. I haven't seen them for nearly five years. Mom kind of decided to forget about me when I got sick."

"Don't you write to her?"

"Some. I don't want her to know where I am. She sends letters through Polly Jo."

"Yeah, I know. That seems dumb."

I felt a little bit annoyed. What did he know about my problems with my mom. But I didn't say anything. Instead I asked him about himself. "What about you? I didn't know you were coming home so soon."

He laughed. "That's the army for you. Three weeks ago I got word to pack my bags and get to Bremen—no explanation about where I was going. It wasn't till I was on that troop ship that I really believed I was headed for home. I got stateside four days ago and sat on my suitcase most of the way home on the train. I couldn't wait. I just grabbed the first train coming this way."

"I'll bet your folks were excited."

"Yeah, I think my Mom still thinks she's dreaming. She's been cooking up a storm ever since I got here." He patted his stomach with one hand. "I'm getting so fat none of my clothes will fit."

I looked at him again. He looked fine to me, not fat at all. Kind of cute, in fact. Made me feel sort of shivery. I looked out the window and didn't say anything. We were driving through flat countryside with lots of little houses and dirt roads without curbs. The houses were new and a lot of them looked alike.

"Where are we?" I finally asked.

"You'll find out in a minute." Jimmy told me. He stopped at a corner by a drive-in. "You want something to drink?" He started to pull in.

"Sure," I said, not knowing what else to say. "Whatever you want."

He pulled up to a menu sign and rolled down his window. A carhop in a short red checkered skirt ran over and leaned down to take his order. When she saw who it was her voice got all flirty

"Hi there," she said practically into his ear. "What can I do for you?"

Jimmy leaned back against the seat and sort of smiled at her. His voice changed too.

"Hi," he said back. "I'll have a chocolate malt. What'll you have, Betsy?"

I wasn't at all hungry but I wanted to be polite so I said I'd have the same thing. The car-hop just stood there for a minute with her elbows on the window, as if she hadn't quite heard what Jimmy said, then she took all the time in the world to write it on her pad, and then she stood back up really slowly, so that Jimmy got a good long look at her front.

"Okaaay," she drawled, and then sauntered over to the restaurant, swinging her hips as she walked.

Jimmy watched her every inch of the way and by the time he got his eyes back into the car I felt like crawling into a hole.

"Well," he said sort of self-consciously. "So…we're going to have some shakes. That'll be good."

And then he cleared his throat and wiped his mouth, as if that would make his grin disappear. I felt awful. I was so flat and skinny I could have cried. My legs were like sticks; all those years in bed had dried up all my muscles and I wasn't round in any of the right places. I thought to myself that no boy would ever look at me the way Jimmy had just looked at that girl.

*   *   *   *

Jimmy took me to his parents' house. When I saw where I was I was so glad I didn't know whether to laugh or cry. Mr. and Mrs. Williams threw their arms around me and we all laughed and cried and hugged.

"Betsy, Betsy, Betsy I can't believe it," Mrs. Williams said, and then she pushed me out to arm's length and said, "Let me look at you! You've put on a little weight I think. You actually look better." And then she started to cry again. "Betsy, do you know how worried we all were? We thought you would kill yourself, running off like that." But her voice didn't sound as scoldy as her words, and when she hugged me again I hung on tight and felt comforted and loved.

It was a little house where you walk right into the living room from outside. Compared to Mrs. Boyle's, things looked new and tidy. I noticed that there were pictures of Jimmy and Polly Jo on the radio cabinet. I just stared and stared at the one of Polly Jo. It seemed like I hadn't seen her in such a long time.

Mrs. Williams saw me looking at it and put her arm around me. "She's coming home before Christmas, honey. Isn't that wonderful?"

I got all teary again. I was embarrassed.

Mrs. Williams took me over to the couch and sat us down so that she was facing me, holding both my hands. "Betsy, we'd like you to come here and stay with us. When Jimmy told us he was going to see you, my husband and I talked it over and we decided that if you were willing it would make us awfully happy to have you here. You and Polly Jo can be roommates just like the old days." Mrs. Williams' neat round little face was just as sweet and kind as I could ever imagine a person to be.

I looked at Jimmy. He smiled at me and nodded his head up and down like he was cheering for me, and his dad nodded at me too, only in more of a questioning way. "Whaddya say?" he asked me.

I thought about Polly Jo. While I was in the hospital I felt as though everything about it was awful, but I remembered the fun she and I had when we roomed together and I was so lonesome for her. She made me feel brave. She always knew what to do. If it wasn't for her I'd probably be lying in bed with my chest all caved in. Then I thought about the police and the law and I remembered how careful I had been to keep everything a secret. I thought to myself, this is the first place they will look for me after Polly Jo comes home. I told Mrs. Williams that.

"Oh honey," she said. "You can't hide forever."

But I realized I could hide for a long, long time if I had to, especially if they would help me.

"I'd just love to be here," I said, "but I'm actually in a good place. I work for my landlady and she is sort of like a mother to me. Really. She's been so nice, and I don't think she'd understand if I just suddenly up and left."

That brought up the subject of my own mother. The Williams had met her once I think.

Mr. Williams said to me, "Betsy, she must be worried about you. Have you talked to her at all?"

He was frowning a little. I shook my head.

"Why don't you call her? We'll be glad to pay for it."

It was a surprisingly scary idea. I guess I hesitated too long, because Jimmy chimed in to say, "Hey, Betsy, she's your mom. C'mon. You've only got one mom."

He went over to the phone. "What's the number? I'll dial."

So I told him, and sure enough, she was at home. When Jimmy handed me the phone my heart was really pounding.

My mother turned out still to be my mother. She said, "Well for heaven sakes, speak of the devil," which seemed like a funny thing to say.

"How are you, Mom?" I said. "Thanks an awful lot for the money. I couldn't have gotten along without it."

"Betsy, you are in a lot of trouble," she said. "The police are looking for you."

I was dumbfounded. Was that all she could think to say to me? I might be dying for all she knew.

"Yes, Mom, I know. They would lock me up if they found me, did you know that? Is that okay with you?" I was starting to get angry until I looked at Mr. Williams who put a finger over his mouth and shook his head no.

"Well, Mom, I'll pay you back the money when I get well enough to get a job. So don't you worry about me, okay?"

"Where are you staying?" she asked me. "Aren't you ever going to tell us?"

"Mom, hardly anybody knows where I am. That way nobody else can get in trouble."

I wondered if she had heard me. She didn't say anything. Pretty soon she said in a funny voice, "Well, Betsy, it was good to hear your voice. You take care of yourself."

And then we said goodbye and I hung up the phone. I had the most awful feeling, empty inside and like I remember feeling when my Daddy left home. Just awful. I looked at Mrs. Williams.

She didn't notice that anything was wrong I guess, because she said, "There. Aren't you glad you did that?"

I just smiled and nodded and didn't say anything.

$$* \quad * \quad * \quad *$$

Jimmy took me home after a little while—Mrs. Williams wanted to feed me supper but Mrs. Boyle was expecting me and I didn't want to worry her any more than I had. We didn't talk very much on the way home. I was still feeling funny from the phone call and from seeing the Williams. I kind of forgot that Jimmy made me nervous, so when we got to Mrs. Boyle's I was surprised when Jimmy said, "Can I see you again?"

I think I had just assumed that once he had talked to me that would be that. But I said any time was all right with me and when he let me out of the car he said he'd like to take me to a movie on Saturday night.

Before I thought what I was saying I said, "I guess that would be a real date wouldn't it?" and then I suppose I blushed because Jimmy really did laugh at me that time.

Then he said softly, "Yeah, we'll have a real date."

I stared at him 'cause by then he wasn't laughing. Oh but I did feel queer.

Mrs. Boyle was on her feet in the hallway waiting for me, her hands on her hips, her grey hair flying every which way, and her eyes alert. "Well young lady, suppose you tell me what is going on? Where did you think you were going without so much as a how-de-do?"

I realized she was mad at me—I thought it was wonderful. I put a hand over my mouth so she wouldn't see me smile and then I said as seriously as I could, "I'm sorry, Mrs. Boyle. I should have told you what was happening." I told her a little bit about who Jimmy was and where I'd been.

She narrowed up her eyes and studied me. "Jan," she said. "When are you going to tell me the whole story. That young man called you Betsy something or other. Is that your real name? I knew it wasn't really Jan. Why couldn't you tell me?"

I looked at her. She had been so wonderful to me. She had had such a hard life. I decided I owed her the truth. I would have given her a hug only she wasn't that kind; she would have been uncomfortable. Instead I just motioned her into the kitchen where we could have a visit. I took off my coat and sat down at the table. Mrs. Boyle warmed up the coffee, poured us each a cup, and then sat down opposite me. She still looked stern. "All right, now," she said. "Suppose you start talking."

I chuckled. "You sound like a radio detective." Mrs. Boyle didn't think it was funny. "Okay," I said. "Do you want the whole story?" Then I sighed. I didn't know where to start. I decided to tackle the hardest part first. "What do you know about TB?" I asked her.

"TB? I had TB once when I was younger. Was out at the county san. Best vacation I ever had. You don't mean to tell me that you have TB?" She put a hand to her cheek like one of those cartoons of surprised people. "Well my land," she said. "Is that what was wrong? But you could have told me about that."

I was thunderstruck. All this time I had been so careful not to mention what was wrong with me and it turns out Mrs. Boyle was a consumptive herself! Amazing. Well then, there was no point in trying to hide anything else, though when I got to the part about my mother she was awfully quiet. I couldn't tell what she was thinking—probably that I was a terrible daughter.

"Have I told you about my daughter?" she said finally. Her face was so sad. I shook my head. "She would be older than you. Twenty eight by now." Mrs. Boyle took a deep breath and pinched her mouth with her fingers. When she was steadier she said, "She died in the polio epidemic of forty-three. She was your age when she died." I could see tears starting, but she squeezed her eyes shut and when she opened them they were dry. "Well," she said. "Her name was Judy. I don't speak of her."

"I'm so sorry, Mrs. Boyle." I didn't know what to say. I didn't want to make her cry again. "I'm glad you told me. I wondered if you didn't have family somewhere."

"Nobody else, you know. My husband was killed in the war. In Italy. My people have been gone for years. Left me this house. That's all. I get by. But it's been nice having you around...what shall I call you? Betsy?

We sat and sipped our coffee and didn't talk. I thought how I had learned to love that kitchen and that house. I thought maybe Mrs. Boyle would like to know that, if I could say it in a way that didn't sound too mushy.

"This is my home now, Mrs. Boyle." I looked at my hands. "I feel like I've adopted you?"

Mrs. Boyle scowled. I could see she didn't approve. "You already have a mother. It isn't right to forget that."

"Maybe you could be my adopted aunt." I tried a tiny little smile to see if she would mind.

A little smile appeared briefly on her face too and then quickly faded. "Well, she said seriously," my name is Elfreda." She thought for a minute. "I suppose you could call me Aunt Elfreda?"

I could see by the seriousness of the question that she was afraid I wouldn't want to. I tried to answer as seriously. "We would both have new names, wouldn't we? I'd be Betsy and you'd be Aunt Elfreda." I couldn't help it, a grin just popped onto my face. "Let's write it down. I'll spell out my whole name and say that I am formally requesting that you and I will be aunt and niece. Then we can sign it."

Mrs. Boyle looked reflective. "That would mean you could have my house when I'm gone," she said.

"Oh no." I hadn't meant that at all. "Oh my goodness no. Oh dear, I'm sorry. No I won't write it down. It's just a game, really...I didn't mean anything serious by it."

Now Mrs. Boyle's eyes were really full of tears. She didn't even try to stop them. "Yes, I would like to write it down. We can be partners. If you know you are going to inherit this house, you won't mind working here, and it will mean so much to me to know that the state won't get it. I think about that sometimes." She studied me shyly. "I pretend you're my daughter, you know."

I reached out my hands to her. I was just as choked up as I could be. Mrs. Boyle covered my right hand with both of hers. Her hands had big swollen knuckles and felt like sandpaper but to me they were like a mother's kiss. I don't suppose anybody ever made me feel better than Mrs. Boyle did just right then.

It was about five o'clock and the kitchen was starting to get dark. I looked out the window at the squirrels running up the oak tree and at the almost falling down old garage and I sneaked a little day-dream; someday this will be mine. But then that made me feel so guilty I squashed it right away and instead I thought; this really is my home for as long as I want to be here. I'll make sure that she never ever is sorry.

I told Mrs. Boyle—"Aunt Elfreda" (we started practicing with our new names)—about my date with Jimmy and she got real serious. I could see she wanted to give me a bird and bees speech so I just said that I might have been out of circulation but I did know what I needed to know and then she was embarrassed.

So she said, "You'll need something to wear."

I started to say no, but she told me to wait a minute and left the room. When she came back she was carrying a big cardboard box which she put down on the table.

"Betsy, I saved some of Judy's things. Let's see if they fit you. She was just about your size."

I could tell that it was hard for her to take the lid off that box. Finally she took a deep breath and opened it. I saw folded up sweaters and skirts mostly, and on top a blue silk blouse and a couple of slips.

"I gave her that blouse," Aunt Elfreda explained. "She had blue eyes."

I didn't know if that meant she wanted me to try it on or not, but when she lifted it up and shook it out I decided she did. So right there in the kitchen I took off the shirt I was wearing and put on the blue blouse. It had a tie at the neck and puffed sleeves. I loved it.

"Go look in the mirror," Aunt Elfreda said. "You look fine.

So I went upstairs to the bedroom and looked at myself. My eyes were blue too, and the blue blouse made them look like fiery little jewels in my face. I pinched my cheeks to make them pinker and I combed my hair. I smiled at myself. I could almost imagine that I looked pretty if you didn't have to look at the rest of me, which I didn't have to do because it was a high mirror. I studied myself. A skinny Grace Kelly, I decided. Or maybe Joan Fontaine. I sucked in my cheeks. There. That was more sophisticated. I pulled my long hair back and twisted it. No, that made me look like a librarian. Maybe I could get Aunt Elfreda to give me a home permanent sometime; they were just new and I had heard that everybody was trying them. I would set my hair and not take the curlers out till Saturday afternoon, and I would hope it wasn't raining so my hair wouldn't come down. I was finally going to go on a date. I squeezed my hands into fists and hugged myself.

*   *   *   *

When the time finally came I was nearly numb with excitement. I was ready at least an hour early and then I had to sit in the livingroom and hope that I wouldn't mess myself up. When it got to be 8:00 and Jimmy still hadn't come I began to wonder if maybe I remembered the time wrong, and at 8:10 I thought, Well maybe he's standing me up, and at 8:35 I thought, Well maybe I should just get out of these clothes and forget it.

Periodically Aunt Elfreda would stick her head around the door and tell me how nice I looked and don't worry about it, he'll be here soon, which for some reason didn't make me feel better. Every time car lights would flash by from the street I'd think, there he is. Once I got up and started for the door, but it was just someone using our driveway to turn around in. So when he finally did come at twenty minutes of nine I had just about given up.

When I opened the door for him he looked kind of surprised. "Gee," he said. "You look really nice." He looked at himself. "I'm sorry I didn't get dressed up. It's just a movie. I hope you don't mind."

I could have died. He must have been able to see how inexperienced I was. I wanted to run right upstairs and put on my jeans again, but of course I couldn't do that, so I tried to remember my Joan Fontaine look and said as smoothly as I could manage, "That's quite all right. Shall we go?"

It was pretty much an awful evening. Neither of us could think of anything to talk about, and it was a dumb Abbott and Costello movie that made Jimmy laugh really loud and that I didn't think was funny. So when it was over he didn't even invite me for a coke or anything, but just hurried me home and said goodnight in the car.

I said "Thank you for a nice time," and walked into the house by myself. I felt like crying but I didn't, and when Aunt Elfreda came down to see who it was, I realized I was home at eleven o'clock. She didn't say a word. I'm sure she could figure it out.

*   *   *   *

So then I didn't hear from Jimmy again for a long time. But in the middle of December I got a phone call from Polly Jo. It was the first time I had heard her voice since August.

"Hi Bonesy, guess who?" her familiar voice said.

I was too surprised to say anything more than, "PJ? Is that you?"

"That's right," she said, "I'm home. I'll bet you didn't think you'd hear from me so soon, did you? Well, I talked Dave into letting me out early. Bones, can you come over? My brother could get you. Could you come and stay for a couple of days? Please. My Mom and Dad say please too. Nobody's looking for you anymore—they've got other people to torture."

I was out of breath just listening to her. She was really cranked up. "Polly Jo, calm down," I said. "Yes, sure, I'd love to see you today." I thought for a minute and tried to make my voice very matter of fact. "If Jimmy can pick me up, I'll be ready in an hour." Then it came to me what was happening and I couldn't stay so cool. "Oh Polly Jo, are you really home? I can't believe it. I have so many things to tell you we'll be up all night."

Polly Jo's voice laughed. "Just like old times, honey."

My second trip out to the Williamses was a lot different from the first. I wasn't going to let Jimmy know I cared anything about what had happened on our date, so I was hard boiled and devil-may-care when he got to the house. I wouldn't let him carry my suitcase and I mostly didn't talk in the car. Finally he quit trying to talk to me too, and his face was stony and grim. I didn't care if he didn't like me. There were other boys. I had lots of time. Also I had had lots of practice with nasty feelings. I knew how to keep them from licking me by thinking about other things, which is what I did that day. I thought about seeing Polly Jo and eating Mrs. William's food and getting lots of hugs. I didn't have to think about Jimmy if I didn't want to, so I didn't.

Polly Jo was lying on the couch when we walked into the Williams' living-room. She had on jeans and a big man's shirt and somebody had cut her hair real short so she looked like Mary Martin did in South Pacific. She jumped up when she saw me and I was amazed at how little she was—I suppose she hardly came to my chin.

She noticed it too, and after we had hugged each other, she looked at me and laughed. "My gosh, Bonesy, I forgot you were so tall. Isn't this funny? I think of you as being just a little bit bigger than I am." She flopped back down on the couch. "Sorry. I only have an hour of up-time. What about you? How much are you up?"

I had to think for a minute. Of course I knew that at the hospital they got you up ten minutes at a time, and then increased it by ten minutes a week, so that it would have taken Polly Jo six weeks to be up an hour; probably by now she was up half an hour twice a day and maybe was allowed to walk around for ten minutes or so only. It was very regimented. But since I had to be up when I had to be up, I never timed myself.

"I try to lie down as much as I can," I said. "I'm just careful, that's all. I take a long nap everyday and I go to bed early, but I walk around some too."

I realized that, in fact, the last time I was at the Williams I hadn't lain down for about four hours. That made me a little nervous to think about. Polly Jo brought back all the warnings they used to give us at the hospital. Like never stand when you can sit, never sit when you can lie down. I tried to remember that.

Mrs. Williams had her arm around my waist—she was little too—and while Polly Jo and I were talking about up-time she looked around the room, which only had a couple of not very lying down chairs in addition to the couch.

"Well, now, let's see," she said. She studied the situation. "James," she said to Mr. Williams, "what would you think of putting the folding cot in here and then both girls can stretch out and talk without using up any of their precious time."

I started to protest that that wasn't necessary, but Mr. Williams paid no attention and pulled a narrow folded up bed from the hall closet. He undid it and pulled the two ends down so that there was a nice little bed against the wall across from the couch. It already had sheets on it and Mrs. Williams ran into the bedroom and came back with two fat pillows.

"There." She turned again to me. "Take off your shoes and make yourself comfortable. Jimmy will take your bag into Polly's room. For now we will say that's Betsy's cot."

So for the weekend, Polly Jo and I took over the Williams' living-room. We propped ourselves on our elbows facing each other and we just talked and talked. Polly Jo told me all about what was happening at the hospital. She said a few people including Marcella were getting shots now; something called streptomycin that was like penicillin. Also they were easing up on a few of the rules. There were visiting hours two times a day instead of just once and people were being allowed to get up a little bit more. She said there were rumors that Sue Ellen had gone out west and was having a baby. Rachel, one of the regular nurses, had told her about it and also that Dave and his wife had separated…you could think what you wanted about that. Personally Polly Jo still didn't believe those stories and she told Rachel so.

As for herself, she was thinking about going to business school next fall because they told her nursing was out of the question. "I feel bad about that, Bones. I can't think of myself as anything but a nurse. It's all I ever wanted to do."

I said maybe she shouldn't decide quite so soon what she was going to do. "Maybe those shots will turn out to be really a cure and you can be a nurse after all."

She said the shots weren't expected to help cases like hers; just really bad cases like Marcella's. Still you never knew.

That night, while we were waiting to go to sleep in the twin beds in her room, we talked in the dark about more important things like getting married and having babies. That was such a big worry to me. Could I ever have a baby? Polly Jo just thought it was silly to worry about it. She planned to have a bunch of kids. She said the docs told her it wasn't any more strain on you than just ordinary living. That didn't make sense to me but I was sure willing to believe it if I could. She told me that Dave was coming to see her sometime soon and did I want to come over too. She made it sound like more than a plain house call, so I asked her what was going on.

Her voice sounded soft and dreamy when she answered. "He's wonderful, do you remember? I know he likes me; he spent lots of time in my room. I think maybe he more than likes me." She sighed.

"Polly Jo, his life is awfully complicated. Don't you think you're taking a big chance."

She brushed my concern aside. "It's nothing, Betsy. He's probably just a friend. I'm being silly." I heard her settling into her covers. "Let's go to sleep. We'll talk more in the morning."

*   *   *   *

I'll bet I gained five pounds that weekend. Mrs. Williams gave us pancakes and sausage for breakfast and a big dinner at noon and then supper of sandwiches with oceans of mayonnaise and fresh cake with frosting plus ice cream. Maybe it was because she cooked for men too that it seemed like so much more than Aunt Elfreda and I ate.

Jimmy made himself scarce the first day, but after supper Friday night he got interested in our conversation about the hospital, and pretty soon he asked us if we wanted to play canasta, which sounded like fun. So we spread the game out on the floor, and we put our pillows there too, and we all laid on our stomachs and played till nearly midnight. I was the big winner and Jimmy came in second, and by then we had both forgotten that we felt strange about each other. Before Jimmy stood up when we were done he squeezed my hand and told me I was a good canasta player.

I went over to the Williams a couple times a month at least after that and I always stayed all night. But after they got to know Aunt Elfreda they stopped insisting I live with them. Still, there was one subject no one seemed to be able to let go of. I starting I hearing about it from everyone. Aunt Elfreda said that with Christmas coming my mother must be wondering more and more where I was. I knew she thought about Judy and about how she would feel if Judy was alive but she didn't know where. She would drop hints every time we spent some time talking.

"You know," she would say with a little sigh. "It's not easy being a mother. Children don't understand."

Or she would say, "I wonder if your mother has your photograph out where she can see it."

She found Judy's high school graduation picture and put it on the mantle, even though I know it hurt her to look at it, and even though people said, Who's that? That picture scolded me every time I walked into the livingroom.

Mrs. Williams wasn't half so subtle. She began asking me when I wanted to go to see my mother and finally, about two weeks before Christmas, she laid a calendar in front of me and said calmly, "Choose a date. We're going to spend a day. James will take time off from work. Betsy, this is something you have to do. I don't want any arguments."

So in the end we went on December 20th. I called my mother a few days before and asked her if it was okay. She was as unenthusiastic as I would have expected, but Mrs. Williams said well, she just wasn't one to show her emotions. I couldn't disagree with that. I told Mom we would get to Pine Center by ten in the morning and that I had to be back by early afternoon so I could take my nap.

Wouldn't you know that we would have a big snowstorm that day. Mr. Williams didn't think Polly Jo should take chances in that weather, so even though she sputtered about it, she stayed home. So just Mr. and Mrs. Williams and I drove away from Aunt Elfreda's house in the Williams' old green Nash. They all fussed and fussed at me; Aunt Elfreda and the Williams were really big pals by then; sometimes I felt like I had more parents than I really needed, only of course I loved it.

They wanted me to look wonderful for my mother, so out came the Judy box and I was fixed up with a pink sweater and skirt and matching socks; I looked like a college student, which was the idea. They wanted my mother to see right away that I was getting well and that I was in good hands.

It took us three hours of straight driving north. There weren't any freeways in those days, so we went through all the Christmasy little towns at fifteen miles an hour and crept along the two-lane country roads with the windshield wipers flopping away at the snow, which mostly was too heavy to be kept pushed aside. It made the trip seem like an adventure into another world. When I saw the Pine Center sign, "Welcome to the Christmas Tree Center of the Midwest," I felt like I was in a dream. The familiar streets were hidden under the big soft snow blanket and I couldn't see any people. It was lucky that that part of the state is so flat, because if we'd had to cope with any slippery hills we'd have been in serious trouble.

My mom's house had been painted gray since I last saw it five years before. I always thought of it as white. She didn't have any Christmas lights and the curtains were drawn. It was a middle aged house with three stories and a steep roof with gables in it. My old room was under the gable above the front door; I wondered who used it these days. My two brothers had the third floor room and my mom used the back bedroom on the second floor.

When I told Mr. Williams to stop, he asked me if I wanted him to come in with me. I started to just say, "No I'm fine," but then I got really scared. I looked at the Williams and felt frozen in my seat. I stared at the house. I felt like I was fourteen again and I wasn't sure what I was scared of.

"Could you just stay here in the car till I'm inside the house?" I asked hesitantly.

"Sure, honey. Of course. You're sure you don't want us to walk you to the door. We could meet your mother. She might like to see who's taking care of you."

I wasn't sure why, but I knew that wasn't a good idea. "Will you be back at noon? I'll be watching for you."

Mrs. Williams wasn't convinced. "Betsy, why don't we call before we come. You may want to stay for lunch, honey."

"No, I don't think so." I didn't intend to sound so stubborn, but I was sure I wouldn't want to stay.

It was a mile up that front walk—somebody had just shovelled it, so at least I didn't have to wade through the snow. I didn't have a key anymore so I had to ring the doorbell. When the door opened there was a tall, thin young man standing there. He had horn-rimmed glasses on and he looked familiar, but I wasn't sure who it was.

"Betsy?" he said, frowning. I didn't indicate I knew him so he said, "It's Joey, Betsy. Don't you know me?" He looked scared and he didn't invite me in. We stood looking across the doorway at each other. Joey. It was my brother. I knew he was twenty now but for some reason I'd forgotten that twenty year olds are men. He was a skinny little fifteen year old the last time I saw him.

"Yeah," I said. "Can I come in?"

He looked embarrassed. "Oh. Sorry." He held the storm door for me and I stepped into the dark hallway. We stood there.

"You've changed," he said. "You look okay. How are you?"

"I'm okay I guess. You've changed too."

"I suppose so."

"Where's Tony?" Tony was my youngest brother. He'd be sixteen by that time.

"Tony doesn't live here any more."

For some reason that didn't surprise me. Tony had been a handful. I had lots of memories of pulling Tony off table tops when he was a baby and out of trees when he got older, and I remembered that there were lots of phone calls from school about Tony. I was like a second mother to him and I liked him even though Mom didn't. At first when I was in the hospital, I worried about him. Mom yelled at him a lot and it made her mad when I asked about him, so pretty soon I quit asking. If he left home I didn't blame him.

"Where's Mom?" My voice was really small.

"She's in the kitchen." Joey looked at me as though he was trying to decide how much to say. "She's not in very good shape."

"She's sick?" We were beginning to sound like characters in a radio soap opera.

"Let's go into the livingroom first, okay? Maybe we'd better talk before you see Mom."

He led the way into that gloomy livingroom which still looked exactly the way it had five years earlier. There weren't any Christmas decorations and it didn't look like anyone ever came in there. He sat down on the brown over-stuffed arm chair with the little doilies on the arms and I sat down on the couch that matched it. He looked owlish in his glasses and as if he'd forgotten how to smile. He sat up very straight. It was like we were having an interview.

"How much have you heard from Mom?" he asked me. "What was going on when you left?"

I didn't know what he meant. "She doesn't know where I live. I've talked to her on the phone but she didn't seem very glad to hear from me." My voice was tight. I cleared my throat. "What's wrong with her?" I was having a little trouble breathing.

"You don't know? Wasn't it going on when you were at home?"

"What? I don't know what you're talking about." I wanted to run for the front door before the Williams left. I could hear Mr. Williams start the car.

"Mom drinks, Betsy. She's been at it all morning. Your coming here really threw her for a loop. She's pretty well out of it." Joey looked apologetic. "I'm sorry. That's a bum homecoming."

I couldn't think of anything to say. I looked at the clock. It was only ten fifteen. What would I do till twelve? I looked at Joey. He was wearing navy blue pants and a white shirt. His brown hair was slicked back. He looked like an accountant. He looked like our dad.

"What do you do, Joey? Do you work?" I decided that we might as well talk since I wanted to stall about seeing Mom.

Joey got up and stepped out into the hall. I saw him stand still and listen, then he walked back in and sat down again. "I don't think she heard you come. She's probably forgotten what's going on."

"What do you mean? Can't she remember things?" I wasn't familiar with people who drank too much.

Joey put his elbows on his knees and rested his face in his hands. He looked like a kid again. He studied me. "Boy, oh boy," he said earnestly. "I don't know where to start. It's a rough business."

He looked off to his right and sort of cranked himself up to begin. I settled back and waited. He reached in his shirt pocket and pulled out a pack of cigarettes. He offered me one. I wasn't smoking much any more, but that day I took one and when he lighted a match, he held it under my cigarette and then lit his. It was nice, sitting there with my brother smoking those cigarettes. Calmed us both down.

"When you went to the hospital, Mom went kind of crazy. She made up all kinds of stories. First she told us you had gone away to school, but Tony and I figured out that you were having a baby. I hear that's what lots of people thought, 'specially when you didn't ever come home. Mom talked about Whitey, that guy that used to work on the house. He wasn't around anymore and he always was strange, so Mom connected Whitey with you."

"I liked Whitey," I said defensively. "He was nice to me. He taught me how to hang wallpaper." I remembered a slight, blonde guy with white eye lashes and pink skin, who put up our storm windows and cleaned out our furnace and painted whatever needed painting. "I wonder how Mom afforded Whitey. I didn't think she ever had extra money. That's what she always told us."

"I doubt that she needed money to pay Whitey." Joey didn't smile.

I thought about what Joey had said. "Do you know now why I went away?"

"Yeah. Aunt Janine told us finally. Made us promise we wouldn't let Mom know we knew."

"Why? Because of Dad? That never made sense to me."

Joey came close to smiling; he let his face twitch and then said seriously, "Don't you understand that Mom doesn't make sense? Did she make sense when you lived at home?"

Did she make sense? I thought about it. She never talked to me. How did I know. She made me feel like I was invisible sometimes—ignored me. I thought I was probably a bad person, only I mostly couldn't think what I had done. But then, kids do bad things. You find out later that they were bad. When I got sick, I guess I thought it figured. I wouldn't ever have thought there was something weird with my mother. At least not at first. Later on I started to wonder about that, when I listened to other people talk about their mothers and when I got to know Mrs. Williams.

"Do you remember the summer after you first went away?" Joey was reminiscing. "Mom must not have visited you for awhile."

I remembered.

"Mom was in the state hospital. She went after herself with a razor blade. Tony found her in the bathroom."

I stared at Joey. I felt sick to my stomach.

He went on. "After she got out she really started the serious drinking."

"What about her job? How can she work?"

"Mom hasn't worked for at least four years. She gets checks from the state. She rents rooms. I help out."

"Joey, why do you stay here? It must be terrible." I couldn't take in all Joey was saying.

Joey looked at me soberly. I noticed how pale he was, like he hadn't been outside, or like he didn't sleep enough. He looked like I used to look. I wondered if he was okay.

"She depends on me," he said. "I keep up the house and I make sure she eats and I pay the bills. I don't know what would happen to her if I wasn't here.

"Did you finish school? Do you work?"

"Oh sure, I finished." He gave me that cracked smile again. "It wasn't easy. I missed a lot of days of class. Do I work? Yeah, I work at the plant. I'm on the midnight shift. It's good money."

"So you just got home from work? Have you been to bed yet?"

"Naw. That's okay. I'll sleep in the afternoon. I usually stay up for a while after I get home. Anyway, I knew you were coming."

I tried to get my thoughts together. "Did you know that Mom sent me money?"

"Of course," Joey said. "It wasn't her money."

"Joey, why didn't you visit me? Why didn't you try to write me?" It suddenly occurred to me that I might have made his life a little easier.

A mask came over his face. His grey eyes were veiled and his words were careful. "I know I should have. I didn't know how sick you were." He stopped. I couldn't tell what he was feeling. "I was already taking care of one sick person," he said without emotion.

I felt so much sadness for him. I thought about the quiet, serious little boy who collected rocks and fossils and whose main interest was making lists and putting his collections in categories. I always assumed he'd be a scientist and I know his teachers thought so too. Here he was only twenty years old and he looked and acted as if he was middle aged. He was three years younger than Jimmy, but he seemed much, much older.

"What about Aunt Janine," I asked. "Didn't she help?" Aunt Janine lived about an hour away.

"Aunt Janine and I don't speak to each other anymore. She thinks I'm wasting my life and she says I should give up on Mom like she's done. She says she's not going to waste any more of her energy on someone who is determined to wreck her own life."

"Oh. Maybe she's right."

"She's not right. Could you live with the idea that Mom killed herself because of you? That's what will happen. Mom says if I ever leave she'll kill herself." Joey's face was flushed. He was upset.

I could see I might as well drop the subject. "Maybe I should go see her," I suggested. I felt tense. My heart was beating really fast.

"Okay. She looks terrible so don't be surprised." Joey's eyes showed a little anger. "I made her get dressed at least. Most of the time she stays in her bathrobe."

We went into the hall together and then Joey led the way back to the kitchen. Mom was sitting at the kitchen table with a glass in her hand. I looked at Joey and nodded toward the glass; I wondered why he let her drink. He shrugged.

She looked up as we came in. She didn't change her expression, which was hard and cross.

"Well, hello there," she said dully. "You're still alive, I see."

Her voice didn't sound like I would have thought a drunk person would sound. It was loud and flat; she stayed on one note, sort of. I realized I had heard her talk that way before.

She didn't look so much sick as she did just disheveled. She had gained weight; I remembered her as being slim, but now she looked puffy, and her hair needed cutting and combing. I recognized the dress she was wearing; she had taken out the hem to make it long enough for the new fashion look and hadn't bothered to rehem it. I was amazed that seeing her didn't upset me much. She was like sides show freak, someone to look at.

"Hi Mom," I said, and I made myself walk over and give her a kiss.

She lifted up her face but she didn't respond any other way. I saw her wipe my kiss away with the back of her hand. Even drunk as she was, I suppose she was afraid she might catch something.

"Let's go," I said to Joey.

Mom just watched me and didn't say anything. I looked back at her. She wanted me to leave. I realized she had looked at me like that lots of times and that probably she had wanted me to leave lots of times. Well, I had left hadn't I? I was lucky.

We went back in the hallway and suddenly I wanted to see the rest of the house. So Joey took me upstairs and we walked slowly through the bedrooms and then up to the third floor. "Nobody's using this floor now," Joey said. "The last renters got sick of Mom's screaming and I haven't tried to find anybody else."

The house was spotless. "I spend a lot of time cleaning," Joey explained. "I feel crazy if the house gets messy. I get after Mom to keep things picked up. Some times she'll help and then some times she fights me. Last week she broke up some chairs."

I said I didn't understand.

Joey looked at me like I had a lot to learn. "She picks up chairs and throws them at the walls. See." He pulled out a desk chair with one leg hanging loose. He sighed. "Look at that wall. See the hole in the plaster? I haven't had a chance to fix it. I'll do it next week."

We sat down on the bed in Joey's room and looked out the window at the snow. He used my old room, and he could look at the telephone poles and the neighbor's chimney just like I used to do.

"Joey do you ever go anywhere? Do you ever get out of here? This is like being in prison. This is worse than the hospital."

"Oh, about once every three months or so we put Mom back in the hospital and then I take a trip or visit friends, that kind of stuff. But when she's home she really needs me to watch over her."

"What about when you work?"

"I work nights, remember? She sleeps a lot even during the day, but at night she watches TV and then goes to bed. If she hasn't gone to the bar by the time I leave for work I know she'll be okay."

I didn't want to talk about it any more. I knew then how Aunt Janine felt. So instead I asked about Tony.

"Oh, he lives with Aunt Janine. She came and got him one time. Said she had a court order. He was mad, I'll tell you. Didn't want to go. After all, he hadn't had anybody tell him what to do for a long time. He'd quit going to school and was hanging out with the punks downtown. Finally he got arrested, and that's when Aunt Janine took him."

"How's he doing?" I realized I wanted to see him.

"Actually he's doing okay. Aunt Janine is tough, just what Tony needed. He gets out of line, she smacks him and makes him stay in his room. He's afraid of her and he likes her. He really likes Uncle Jack too. He's learning to fix cars and helps out at Uncle Jack's garage. He still doesn't go to school, but he's sixteen now, so that's okay."

I wondered if Joey was jealous, but I didn't say anything. I just said I was glad Tony had gotten out of there and I was sorry that Joey was stuck with Mom. I didn't tell him I was glad Mom hated me and didn't want me to stay.

Joey and I were still sitting on the bed talking when I saw the Williams' green Nash pull in to the curb. I went to the window and waved. Mrs. Williams saw me and waved back. She blew me a kiss.

I suddenly thought to myself, What will I tell them? That my mother goes to the state hospital every now and then? That she's an alcoholic? That she hates me? I had to think fast. I would tell them that she wasn't feeling well. I chuckled to myself. Too bad I couldn't use that serum-hematome story anymore. I wondered if Aunt Elfreda would believe me if I made up still another story after I had lied to her for so long. Well it was bad enough to be a consumptive. For sure nobody would like me if they knew I had a crazy mother. Lots of people already thought I was crazy—if they knew about Mom, they'd be sure of it.

"Joey, will you come out to the car with me. I'd like the Williams to meet you. You're nice and normal. But I don't want them to know about Mom, okay? I want them to think Mom has the flu, or a bad heart or something. What do you think?"

Joey was earnest. "A bad heart sounds good. She's in bed because she's had a little spell with her heart."

I laughed. "Oh dear, they'll want me to visit her every week. How'll I get out of that?"

Joey studied the situation. "She needs to be protected from TB," he said seriously. "That's why she didn't see you very often"

Impulsively I put an arm around him. "Oh Joey, I do want to see you again. When are you going to come to see me?"

"I'll come the next time Mom is in the hospital," he promised.

I guess everyone bought my story about my mother. At least there were no more questions and the only talk about her came from Aunt Elfreda, who decided I should write her a letter once a week. She bought me a box of light blue stationery with my initial at the top, and she told me that I should try to write Mom on Sundays. I thought well I would really write the letters to Joey even though they were addressed to my Mom, and I quick wrote him a note telling him to open anything that came from me; I mailed that letter myself so Aunt Elfreda wouldn't see it.

People were interested in my brothers though, and I didn't have to make up too much about them. I made it sound as if Tony was just out of control, which he was, and Joey had to take care of Mom, which he did. The Williams wanted the boys to come down to their house for a few days, and they particularly wanted to meet Aunt Janine. But I knew how Aunt Janine was—she would blurt out everything in the first ten minutes—so I said that she and I didn't get along at all and that was why I never got in touch with her. That wasn't true—Aunt Janine was fine, I liked her—but she wasn't one to cry over spilt milk, as she would say. I'm sure she didn't worry about me, since there wasn't anything she could do about my situation. I decided Joey would let her know how I was getting along, and I didn't think I had to do any more about her than that. But that was too hard to explain to anyone who didn't know Aunt Janine, so I didn't try.

I asked Mrs. Williams if I could start putting their address on my letters. I still was afraid to let anyone know where I really lived, and I decided that if the hospital people or the police got the Williams' address from my family, at least I wouldn't be there when they came looking for me. Mrs. Williams didn't really like the idea—"I'm not a very good story teller," she said—but she tried to understand.

Polly Jo agreed with me. She didn't know whether they could force me to go back, but she thought it was possible. I told her all about my mother; I didn't have any secrets from Polly Jo.

She just listened carefully and when I was done, she said "Bones, I don't know why your mother's the way she is, but it doesn't have anything to do with you, honey. You have a new family and now you're gonna have to let us take care of you. I'm gonna be your sister and you're gonna forget about your Mom and concentrate on getting totally well and having a new life."

It sounded good, but a warning voice inside me said it wasn't going to be that easy.

CHAPTER 4

▼

SEX

Jimmy began to think it was really funny that there were so many things I didn't know about. He loved to tell me about the big city burlesque shows, and about working in the auto plant, and about the newest dances at the dance halls. He said when I was better he would take me to Stoney Lake where all the big bands came to play. He treated me like a little sister, which was okay with me. I finally got over feeling self-conscious when he was around.

All that started to change during Christmas week. Aunt Elfreda and I had everybody over for a big dinner on Saturday afternoon before Christmas Eve. Jimmy and Mr. Williams were off work for the long weekend, so they could "come early and stay late" as they put it. We had put up a tree—Aunt Elfreda said it was the first tree she'd had since Judy died—and since she was Norwegian she fixed cod fish and boiled potatoes and rice pudding for dessert. She put a penny in the rice pudding and whoever got it was supposed to have good luck in the coming year.

We also had whiskey in little glasses before dinner. It didn't seem like there was very much and I didn't finish mine very fast either; even when Aunt Elfreda called us to come to the table I had about half of my whiskey left. Jimmy told me later that when I wasn't looking he kept filling up my little glass, but I didn't see him do it so when I stood up and almost lost my balance I was embarrassed. Everyone else seemed to be fine and when Jimmy put a hand under my elbow and asked me if he could help me, I tried to pretend I wasn't dizzy and could walk without stumbling. He just smiled and said "okay," but then he walked beside me and laughed at me when I kept saying, "I'm fine."

I made it to the table, but I had to concentrate really hard to hear what was being said and a couple of times I didn't quite get my fork to my mouth. When I bit down on something hard in my rice pudding I couldn't think what was going on, and I spat it out with enough force so it went CLINK onto my plate and then bounced onto the floor.

Everybody laughed and applauded and Jimmy bent down and picked up the penny and handed it to me. "Good luck for a year," he announced.

"About time!" I said and everybody laughed again.

After dinner Jimmy told everyone that he was going to take me for a walk to sober me up.

His mother said, "Jimmy! What kind of a thing is that to say?"

Aunt Elfreda thought he was just kidding, but Polly Jo had noticed me staggering around and said, "Bones, do you feel all right?"

I nodded "yes" and then shook my head "no" and then laughed.

Jimmy winked at Polly Jo and said, "Don't you worry, Sis. She'll be safe with me," and helped me on with my coat.

The cold air slammed into me when we went out the door of the porch and I guess I shivered.

Jimmy put his arm around me and then, when I didn't stop shivering, he said, "Here."

He opened up his wool army jacket and took my arm and put it around his waist inside the jacket. Then he wrapped the jacket around us both and held it in place with his arm. It felt lovely and warm and I leaned against him as we started to walk. I wasn't clear headed enough to think about what was happening—it was just my friend Jimmy.

But when we stopped at the corner to wait for the light to change and he put one hand against my face to turn it toward him, I thought, Wait a minute! and started to giggle. Then when he leaned over and tried to kiss me it seemed like a game, so I turned my head the littlest bit. He missed my mouth and caught me on the side of the chin.

Just then the light turned green and we hurried across without saying anything. When we were a few yards further up the street where it was darker he stopped and turned me around inside the jacket so that we were almost facing each other—I was still skinny—and then he really did get a firm grip on my head. This time he didn't miss.

It seems hard to believe these days, but no boy had ever kissed me before. I wasn't a bit prepared for how it would make me feel. I thought my knees were going to give out on me and then I found out I was going to have a terrible time walking.

It didn't matter because Jimmy wasn't going to move. He put his free arm across my shoulder and all the way around my back. I was pressed against him so tightly I couldn't move. Then he kissed me again really hard and before I knew what was happening his mouth was pushing mine open and I could feel his tongue in my mouth. I closed my eyes and let the feelings take over. I don't know why I wasn't scared. I dimly remembered that he had said I would be safe with him and I must have trusted him to take care of me. He was breathing hard, but then so was I.

Finally it must have occurred to him that we were standing on a busy public street, so he let go of me a little and said hoarsely, "C'mon, let's go." We started to walk. By then he wasn't walking very steadily either.

I asked him where we were going.

"Let's go back to the car," he said tensely.

But after we had walked for a minute more I realized what he was suggesting. I was perfectly clear-headed about not being ready for that and I surprised myself by knowing just what to do. I squeezed him with my arm that was around him, and with my face against his cheek—we were nearly the same height—I whispered, "I think I'd better get back to the house. Everyone will wonder where we are."

He tried to argue with me, even tried to pressure me toward the car when we got in front of the house, but I just kept touching my lips to his face and saying firmly, "No, we're going to go inside."

Finally I took my arm back and he snapped his jacket shut and we both combed our hair, and after we practiced looking casual—that made us laugh, which was good. We walked up the steps back onto the porch, opened the door and then strolled calmly into the front hall.

*   *   *   *

After that, Jimmy was the cat and I was the mouse. Whenever I would be alone in a room he would magically appear. I may have known what to do that night on the walk, but I didn't know what to do with kisses on the back of the neck by the refrigerator or arms around me from behind when I didn't even know he was there. I knew I shouldn't let him put his hands on my breasts, but sometimes it felt so nice I didn't stop him. I never said a word about it to Polly Jo. I wasn't sure whether I should be embarrassed or ashamed or what. I just liked it and I didn't want to be talked out of it.

One night I was sleeping over at the Williams and I got up in the middle of the night to go to the bathroom. I didn't turn on any lights and when I tiptoed out of the bathroom, I ran right into Jimmy, who was standing in the hallway. It seemed the most natural thing in the world that he put his arms around me, and it was a minute before I realized that he had hardly any clothes on, just a pair of cotton shorts. His bedroom door was open directly behind him and without a word he pulled me in and so, so softly shut the door.

In those days we thought that people should save sex for marriage, or at least that's what I thought. But also I wasn't too sure what would get a girl into trouble and what wouldn't. Jimmy had been all over the world, I told myself that he knew what he was doing. When I think about it now and realize that Polly Jo's bedroom was just on the other side of a thin wall, I'm amazed that I let him do what he did. But then I'm not being truthful, because I did it just as much as he did.

Jimmy was quick and quiet and gentle. He never hurt me, not even that first time, and then whenever I slept over we met at that same time, or I would creep into his room and stay for just a little while—Polly Jo would think I was in the bathroom if she woke up—and then go back to my own bed. During the day I didn't think much about it. It was something that happened at night; didn't have to do with my regular life.

*   *   *   *

I first missed my period in March. I still was so sure that Jimmy wouldn't get me in trouble that I decided I was just late. But then in April I started to feel funny in the morning and one morning I threw up. Aunt Elfreda always got up at about six, so there was no way I could be sick without her knowing about it. She heard me, and when I came downstairs for breakfast she frowned at me and looked worried.

"You eat something that didn't agree with you?" she asked me.

I said I guessed so, but when it happened again the next morning, and then again the next, she was good and suspicious. Finally we had it out. By then I was really, really scared and ashamed.

"All right, Betsy," she said after the fourth morning. "What's going on? You'd better tell me."

I didn't cry. I thought to myself, Well this is what happens when you take in a girl you don't know anything about. She turns out to be a tramp. Poor Aunt Elfreda. She'll want me to leave of course. Well that's okay.

Aunt Elfreda poured me a cup of coffee. "Can you still drink coffee? Coffee was one of the first things I had to give up. Just the smell made me sick."

I couldn't believe what she was saying. She poured herself a cup and then sat down. "How far along are you? How many periods have you missed?" She didn't smile but then she didn't look mad either.

"How did you know? I don't know myself. Aren't you mad?"

She studied me. "Betsy, some things never change. I've watched you and Jimmy. I suppose I should have said something, but I didn't think it was my business. Did you think you wouldn't get caught?"

I was shocked. Aunt Elfreda had always seemed staight-laced to me. If she knew what I was doing, why didn't she stop me?

"Will Jimmy do the right thing by you?" Aunt Elfreda's jaw was set. "Well of course he will. His parents will see to that."

"Do I have to tell him?" That was a new worry. "Can't I just go away and have it?"

"Go away? Go where? Where could you go? To your mother? Your aunt?"

I stared out the window. Where would I go? Polly Jo couldn't help me this time—she would really be mad. Oh dear, how could I face the Williams?

"You won't tell anybody, Aunt Elfreda. Please. Promise me."

Aunt Elfreda looked disgusted. "See here, young lady. You will take your medicine like a grownup. What you did was wrong, but it was understandable. But now you are going to think of this baby and you are going to start by telling Jimmy that he is going to be a father, and then the two of you are going to talk to his family. Because if you don't, I will."

I started to argue with her—I could think of all kinds of reasons why I couldn't do those things—but she just went right on talking like I didn't have a right to speak.

"Furthermore," she said, "you are going to get yourself to a doctor today. You've done quite enough fooling around with your health. We aren't going to have our baby taking any chances."

I felt like a boat with a tough captain sailing it through a storm. Everything was out of my hands. I basically went where I was told to go and did what I was told to do. Aunt Elfreda made me telephone Jimmy to come over after work, and then she told me she would go to the movies so we could be alone to talk. That made me nervous because Jimmy and I hadn't talked much. Mostly we had been alone in the dark or there had been other people around. I didn't have any idea what he would say, but I thought probably he'd be mad at me.

I think he knew what I was going to tell him. He started to mess around when Aunt Elfreda left for the show—we didn't very often get a chance to have the house to ourselves—but when I said, "No, I have something I need to talk about," he let me go and went and sat by himself in a chair.

I told him I had missed two periods and I thought I was pregnant.

He didn't want to believe me. "Are you sure?" he said. "Have you seen a doctor?"

That seemed like such a dumb question I was stumped to know how to react.

"Of course not," I said. "I'm hiding from doctors, remember?"

"Don't you ever miss periods? I thought girls missed them all the time."

"I'm sick in the morning now, Jimmy. Aunt Elfreda is sure I'm pregnant."

"Oh great," he said sarcastically. "The whole world knows about this, right?"

We didn't say anything for a few minutes. Finally he said, "What are you going to do?"

"Aunt Elfreda says we should talk to your parents."

"Are you crazy? Why would we do that?"

I felt calm and angry. "We're going to get married, Jimmy. I want to have this baby and I'm not going to give it away."

Jimmy glared at me. "Why didn't you tell me you could get pregnant? Do you think I'd have taken chances if I'd known that? P.J. told me you probably couldn't have kids."

I could feel my eyes fill, even though I was saying to myself, Now don't get upset.

"We worried that we couldn't have kids…that they wouldn't let us," I said. "I don't know what will happen to me now. Maybe I'll get sick again. I hope not, but maybe I will. But that doesn't change what's happened, Jimmy. You're going to have to help me, that's all. It's your baby too."

"Oh…" Jimmy cursed. I'd never heard him use that word before. I waited. The electric clock hummed and the house creaked and I felt my heart thumping.

Finally Jimmy said crossly, "Okay, we'll talk to my parents. But I'm not going to take all the blame for this. It was your idea too."

I'd never thought about blaming anyone. "Yes, of course it was my idea too. They'll probably hate me. That's okay. I'll understand."

Jimmy exploded at me. "Damn it, Betsy, are you crazy? Don't be so calm! Don't you know that this could ruin both of our lives. I'm not ready to be tied down to a family. You don't even know if your TB is under control. Who's gonna take care of this kid if you are sick? How do you know the kid won't be sick too?" He looked frantically at the ceiling and shook his fist. "Damn what a mess!"

I said something I shouldn't have. "I guess you should have thought of all that before you started."

*   *   *   *

Mrs. Williams cried. She was the only one who did. Mr. Williams heard our story and his face got white and he excused himself to go outside. Jimmy looked scared when his father did that, but when his mother started to cry he got cross again and said, "Mom, there's no point in crying."

She looked at him, and then she looked at me, and then she said, "Oh Betsy, I'm sorry. I should have known what was going on. I should have prevented it. I could tell that you two were sweet on each other. I guess I just didn't stop to think. I'm so sorry." She took a deep breath and tried to stop crying. We three just looked at each other.

"You'll get married right away," she said. "We'll just say it was a premature birth. Nobody else needs to know."

Jimmy couldn't leave it alone. "Suppose Betsy gets sick again, Mom. Have you thought about that?"

Mrs. Williams looked flustered. "Well of course she's not going to get sick. We're going to take wonderful care of her. She's going to be fine." She came over and put her arms around me. "You're going to be fine, honey." She looked defiantly at her son. "Just think. We're going to have a baby. Isn't that wonderful?"

Dave came over to the Williams's house the next day. Polly Jo called him and told him that we had an emergency and that she needed him. She sounded like a different person when she talked to him, silky and purry; it made me uncomfortable. I was used to the crackly, funny Polly Jo who treated life like a big game.

When I had told her about the baby, she had thrown her hands in the air and done a shaky-shimmy with them. "Whooey me," she said, "ya'll could've fooled me, honey chile." Polly Jo put on her southern mammy act when she wanted to hide her real feelings. "Just think. I could've put my ear to the wall and had a gooood time."

She surprised me. I thought that of all people she would understand, and instead she turned out to be the one who was mad. "Bones," she said when she finally cooled off, "you are a dope."

I said knew that.

"My brother spits out girls like cherry pits. I told him to leave you alone and I guess I should have told you the same thing, only I figured you were so innocent you wouldn't know what I was talking about. What is his problem? Did he think just because your lungs are messed up that the rest of you is too?"

I said that was what he thought.

Polly Jo crunched up her face in disgust. "He's a bigger dope than you are then." She looked thoughtful. "Bones, do you realize that you could be in real trouble? Honey, you may have wrecked yourself good." I wasn't sure what she meant. "I mean your lesion, Bonesy. You've got to see a doctor. You've got to have an Xray."

I told her that Aunt Elfreda had said the same thing but I didn't know who to call.

"Dave," Polly Jo said. "He knows your case. He's sympathetic. He won't blow any whistles on you. We'll call Dave."

So Dave knocked timidly on the Williams' door and then came cautiously in like he didn't know what kind of hornets' nest he was messing with. He didn't see me at first; he shook hands with Mrs. Williams and smiled self consciously at Polly Jo, who looked like butter wouldn't melt in her mouth. When he saw me he just couldn't stop himself from grinning.

Dave is a big, big man and when he grins you can feel waves of niceness all around him. He has shaggy brown hair and a shaggy, loose face. I grinned too. He held out his arms to me and without even thinking about how he was a doctor and I'm scared of doctors, I walked into his. It seemed like those long arms went around me about twice and he hugged me so tightly my breath went out of me with a little gasp.

"Hey, hey, hey," he said when he let me go. "It really is you, Betsy. I thought we'd lost you."

I felt annoyed. "I'm sure you did. I turned out to be tougher than you thought."

It was a snippy thing to say and I was sorry as soon as it was out of my mouth. I wasn't aiming it at Dave especially, but at all of those smart aleck people who had pushed me around. Just seeing Dave made it all come back to me.

We sat down and Dave said, "So, what's going on? Polly made it sound like a crisis situation."

Mrs. Williams excused herself and went out to the kitchen, and Polly Jo looked at me questioningly and then said, "Bones, I think you should talk to Dave alone." She went out to the kitchen too.

Dave cocked his head and studied me. "Okay," he said mildly, "what cooks?"

I couldn't think what to say. It was too long a story, and the part that wasn't too long I didn't want to tell him.

He tried again. "Betsy, how are you? Do you feel all right?" I nodded. "You've gained weight, your color is good, you look fine. Are you having symptoms?" I shook my head. "Something has changed? You're worried about something?" He was fishing.

"I'm pregnant, Dave."

I blurted it out. He tried to look nonchalant, but he put his hand on his forehead as if he might be sweating.

"Gee, is that right?" he said. "Well, well, that's too bad. Hmm. That changes everything doesn't it? Well, let me think about that." He was flustered. He wrinkled the loose skin on his forehead with his raised eyebrows and then pushed it together into a frown. He stroked his chin with his fingers. He didn't look at me.

His discomfort steadied me. "I think I'm about three months along. I feel fine but everyone thought I should see a doctor and I was afraid I would be in bad trouble if I called somebody I didn't know, so Polly Jo suggested calling you. I won't go back to the hospital, Dave. I absolutely won't, so you have to understand that first off."

"You won't, eh? Well you sound pretty determined. Did you think I would try to talk you into going back?"

"Yes that's what I think."

"Hmm. You wouldn't even consider it?"

Just what I was afraid of was happening. "Never mind," I said. "Forget it. I've gotten along by myself this long; I can do it some more. Forget it." I could feel myself clamping down.

Dave pulled himself together and smoothed himself out. "Okay kiddo, I'm sorry. No hospital, okay? I won't even bring it up again. Let's talk about what you're going to do."

"I'm going to get married," I said grimly.

"You're going to have this baby?"

It was my turn to be surprised. "Of course. What else can I do?"

"Waaall," he drawled, trying to sound casual, "in your situation it would be perfectly legal and even advisable to end the pregnancy." He cleared his throat.

"You want me to have an abortion?" I made it sound like an accusation. I was disappointed in him. "No."

I guess he got the picture. He changed the subject. "How long since you've had a chest film, Betsy?"

I told him I hadn't had one since summer.

"I think that's our first step, then. I can order one for you through the county health department. You can use your married name so no one will connect you with our little runaway. When are you getting married? Soon, I hope."

Everything had moved so fast I hadn't even thought about the when of getting married. "This weekend," I said impulsively. "Saturday. I would like you to come."

"Do you mind telling me who the happy bridegroom is to be?"

"Polly Jo's brother. Jimmy Williams."

Dave's face brightened. "Okay. So you will be under the Williams' capable care. That makes me feel more optimistic."

I explained about Aunt Elfreda and how she was like a mother to me, and about all the good care I had had right along, and I could tell that Dave was changing his mind about the seriousness of my crisis.

"That doesn't sound so bad, Betsy. Maybe things will be fine. Let's hope so. But you know, don't you, that you'll have to be careful. Lots and lots of milk and lots and lots of bed-rest. Can you manage that?"

I told him I could.

"I'm going to have to refer you to an obstetrician, okay? Also," he hesitated, "I want a sputum test. Now. Today. I'm going to go back and get a gastric setup. We've got to know if you are contagious."

"Will you give me shots?"

"Probably not if your gastric is negative. We only use the streptomycin on the most critical cases. We'll see what your films look like. By the way, Jimmy should have a film too. Also your aunt should."

I sighed. I felt as though I was back in the old meat grinder. But then I thought about my baby and I realized that I had to do it for him.

"Okay," I said to Dave. "You promise you'll keep me out of the hospital and I'll do what you tell me to."

I felt sad. For six months I had hidden myself from the truth, whatever that turned out to be. I couldn't hide anymore. It didn't feel good.

*   *   *   *

The wedding was quick and businesslike, but everyone was there; that seemed important to me. We got married at the city hall, with the Williams and Aunt Elfreda and Dave standing in a line behind us to be our witnesses. Jimmy didn't even pretend to be a good sport. He snapped out "I do" and mumbled the "I take thee's" and jammed a cheap silver ring on my hand; it was too big and wobbled around for months. Finally it fell off while I was bathing and then I never wore a ring again.

I moved in with the Williams the day after we got married. Aunt Elfreda said that I should try to work things out with Jimmy, but he wouldn't stay in the house with me. I found his mother crying after he left home and I felt bad for her. I tried to think if it was my fault, but I decided it wasn't. I decided he was selfish and mean and his family deserved better; I was always honest with myself about that. I would give them a grandchild but I couldn't transform their son. I was glad I hadn't loved him.

The tests were all negative, so that was a relief and a surprise. Dave sneaked a set of my old X-rays out of the hospital so he could compare them with the new ones, and he said he was amazed at the improvement.

"But the pregnancy will be the big test. For a while you'll continue to improve because the baby will push up your lungs and give them a rest. But the delivery could cause problems. We'll see what the OB thinks."

The obstetrician—Dave called him the "OB"—was very skeptical. He was a white haired doctor who didn't think I should have kids, period. His office was in a different town and Dave sent me with a letter of referral so that all the reports would go to him. The OB gave me a little lecture about responsibility and implied that I should talk to a social worker. It took me a day or so to figure out that he meant I should give my baby away. I was really angry about that. I was married, I had a family, why couldn't I take care of my own baby? But he wanted to talk to my husband, and when no husband appeared I understood that he thought I had made the story up.

Every time I went to see him he talked to me about how he would rather TB patients didn't have babies. Usually I drove home in tears. "What does he want me to do, wear black and tell him how awful I am?" I asked Dave finally. "I hate him. Can't I see someone else?"

But Dave said no, he was competent but lazy, and he wouldn't check up on me so I should keep going to him. "You're the one who wants to hide," he told me. "It's not my idea."

Polly Jo stopped pretending she and Dave were just friends. He had been such a rescuer to me that her family thought he was super-human; they didn't know about his family and Sue Ellen and all. He came over on the pretense of seeing about me, but then he would invite Polly Jo to go for a drive, and either they drove to the next state and back or they weren't spending all that time in the car. Polly Jo would come in looking dreamy and preoccupied and unwilling to answer questions. Since I was the only person who knew about Dave's past, I couldn't ignore the subject. I thought I owed it to everyone to nag at her, so for a while we circled around each other while I waited for a good opening.

Finally I just gritted my teeth and said it. "Polly Jo, what do you know about Dave's wife and kids? What do you know about Sue Ellen? Don't you think having one of us in trouble is enough?"

So that put it out on the table. I waited for Polly Jo to explode, but then she never did react to things the way I expected. Instead her eyes filled up with tears and she let them spill down her cheeks while she answered my question.

"He's going back to them, Bonesy. Next week. His wife found out about Sue Ellen and left him, but he says he made it up to her and when she and his two kids get back from Florida they are going back together. But he wants to go on seeing me too. He's perfectly honest about it. He isn't a sneak. He says he loves us both and he doesn't want to give me up."

"Polly Jo!" I had never been so shocked. "You wouldn't! That's awful."

She put her head down and cried and cried. "He's so wonderful. I've never known a man like him. He's so good to me—takes me wonderful places and treats me like a queen. How can it hurt anything as long as his wife never knows. He says I make him so happy that he is able to be nicer to her. I know that sounds like a big excuse, but I think it must be true. If I don't mind about her, I don't see why she should mind about me."

I stated the obvious. "She's his wife. Anyway, if she doesn't mind, does he tell her? I'll bet he doesn't."

"Oh Bonesy!" Polly Jo looked at me with terrible, terrible pain in her eyes. "I love him so much. I've loved him for three years. I never thought he'd think of me as anything but a patient. This seems like a miracle."

"How did it start? Was this going on in the hospital?"

"Sort of. I asked him about his own TB one time and he spent a long time talking about it. I don't think he had had a chance to really tell anybody the whole story. Not anybody who really understood, at any rate. He would come in and sit by my bed and talk by the hour. Anyway he was lonely, you know? His wife was gone and Sue was gone and he said he felt as though he had messed up his whole life."

"Did he talk about Sue Ellen?"

"Yes, and that really hurt him more than anything. She left without telling him where she was going or what she was going to do. Just walked out on him."

"We heard she had a baby."

"She did, but it wasn't his, and that was the worst part. He said it really killed him."

"Don't you think he spreads himself around maybe too much? I mean, he seems to fall in love awfully easily." I thought I might as well be blunt.

"Bonesy, he's a loving person. You can see that. Look how nice he's been to you. He hasn't sent you a bill. He goes along with you about everything being secret."

I had to admit it. At first I worried about how I would pay my doctor bills, and then I thought maybe the state paid for them—they had paid for my hospital stay after all—but finally I realized Dave wasn't going to charge me anything. The OB was going to charge me five hundred dollars for the whole thing, delivery and all. Aunt Elfreda handed me an envelope with a check in it one morning and told me it was for "our baby." $500. I took it. It was most of her savings.

After that conversation about Dave, things were touchy between Polly Jo and me. I decided that I should go back to Aunt Elfreda's so that if Jimmy wanted to come home he could, and so that Polly Jo couldn't use me as an excuse to see Dave. Anyway, I just didn't want to know about it and I didn't want to answer Mrs. Williams' questions about it. I thought about all the dreams Polly Jo and I had had about falling in love, and it seemed to me that nothing had worked out the way it was supposed to.

CHAPTER 5

▼

RERUN

My pregnancy was uneventful, thank goodness. The nausea passed after the third month and Aunt Elfreda's bossiness kept me quiet and well fed. It was really nice to be taken care of, really odd in fact, and made me realize that that hadn't happened very often in my life. And Aunt Elfreda was excited about "our baby" and I wasn't particularly scared. The OB didn't make me get Xrays because even then they were beginning to worry about what Xrays could do to you—it was 1951 and the Japanese were already starting to have atom bomb sicknesses—but I felt wonderful so I was sure everything was all right.

When my time came I first had a funny back ache in the middle of the night and by morning it wasn't funny anymore. But I wasn't in any hurry to go to a hospital again, so by the time the serious business started we threw my suitcase in Aunt Elfreda's old car and she forgot how cautious she usually was about going fast. By the time we got inside the new women's hospital I was pretty much bent over double, and I couldn't believe it that they made me sign a bunch of documents before they put me in a wheelchair and hurried me upstairs.

In those days you could have what was called a "caudal"—a spinal injection that was supposed to stop the pain—but sometimes it didn't work, in my case probably because the intern who stuck the needle in my tail didn't exactly know how to do it. Anyway, when this huge, enormous urge to push swooped down on me I didn't know what to do because the intern kept saying "don't push, your doctor's not here yet."

When the OB finally came strolling in and said, "Let's get her to a delivery room," I was crazy with the pain of not-pushing. And then when the OB also told me not to push, "we don't want to strain your lungs," I would have started screaming except that just then the caudal kicked in and the pain abruptly stopped. So not pushing wasn't a problem, and in fact I couldn't tell what was going on anywhere below my waist.

I guess the OB sort of dragged the baby out with forceps because she had big welts on her cheeks, but I was too dumb to be worried about that and apparently it didn't do any permanent damage. The OB lifted the baby up to show me that it was a girl, and then whacked her to get her to cry. Then he laid her across my tummy while they went on with business at the far end of me that I couldn't see because they had hung a sheet in front of my eyes. Oh that baby's little bare body felt lovely. Heavy and warm and mine. I was really glad she was a girl because I knew about girls, and I figured I was going to bring up this kid by myself. Jimmy was certainly nowhere in sight. I decided to call her Melissa, a name I'd picked out a long time ago.

In those days, new mothers stayed in the hospital for a week, and in my case they wanted to keep me for ten days "because of your history." But on the third day I was sent down for an X-ray. "to see what kind of trouble you're in," as the OB bluntly put it.

It was only a day later that an obstetrical resident I had never seen before came into my room and sat down by my bed the way they do when something is wrong. At first I wasn't suspicious because I figured if something had turned up either Dave or the OB would be there to tell me. Dave later told me he was so upset he couldn't face me and even the OB wasn't mean enough to be glad it had happened.

They whisked me away into a room by myself and everyone came in wearing masks and gowns—it seemed very familiar. Nobody would talk to me much and I was all alone for hours and hours with nothing to do and no one to answer my questions. I did find out that my baby was "in isolation"—they took her out of the nursery and put her off by herself in case she had TB too. I knew better than to ask to see her.

Finally someone brought me a supper tray which I couldn't eat and I asked if I could use a phone. They said No. I began to tremble really badly and that got a nurse in on the run with a hypodermic. So then my body was calm for a while even though my mind was racing and wild. Where would they send me? What would happen to the baby? Was she all right? Could they make me give her away? Was I going to die?

It was getting dark by the time I heard that they were sending me back to the TB floor. That same resident doctor came in briefly and told me what was happening. He said an ambulance from my old hospital would be there shortly to take me back. They would keep the baby where she was. Who did I want notified? I said please could someone call Aunt Elfreda and then I learned that she had been there but they wouldn't let her see me.

When I look back on that day I wonder why no one was there to help me. Where was Dave? Why wouldn't they let my friends come in? I know now that they were all afraid of me. I was like a leper—everyone was afraid they would catch something. In a TB hospital, people are used to being around a contagious disease. But on an obstetrical ward, a disease like TB is just about the most alarming thing that can turn up. I suppose they panicked—I can't explain to myself in any other way why they were so cruel as to leave me all alone.

Can you imagine how I felt to be back on that same TB floor I had run away from? It was lucky I was in so much shock and that they had pumped me full of dope—I wasn't alert enough to worry about how I would be treated because I had other things to worry about. When they wheeled my stretcher off the elevator I kept my eyes closed and I remember thinking over and over to myself, "I can stand anything if I have to." I heard Miss Ebersole's voice saying "She goes into fourteen" and then they rolled the stretcher to the end of the hall and I heard the orderly asking me if I needed help getting into bed. When I opened my eyes, I found myself in another empty room—no radio, no possessions, nobody to talk to, nothing to do except lie there.

I suppose in my whole life I have never been so glad to see anyone as I was to see Dave that night, after the supper trays had been picked up. He strolled in without a mask on, which was totally against the rules, and when he sat down next to my high bed he put his elbows on it and I could see that he was crying. He took my hand and held it for a few minutes. I was still so calm from the second hypo they had given me that I couldn't cry. It was a terrible feeling—my mind was crying but my body couldn't.

"What have they told you?" Dave asked me finally.

"Nothing. I haven't talked to anyone." My voice was small and dry.

He sighed and put his other hand over mine too. "I looked at the Xray, Bonesy." His using my nickname felt comforting. "Your left lesion has broken down. It looks absolutely fresh. I suspect it happened this week when you delivered."

I asked the question that had been most on my mind. "Is my other lung okay?"

"So far the right side looks stable. It's hard to know for sure."

"So now will I have to have a thoracoplasty?" I surprised myself with that calm question.

"Well actually, maybe not. I know you aren't feeling very lucky, but in fact you may turn out to be luckier than you know. We'll start you on streptomycin this week and maybe that will do the trick."

I felt really scared. I remembered that streptomycin was only for the worst cases. Was that me?

"Dave," I asked carefully. "Will I be okay? Have I finally gone and done it?"

Dave put my hand up to his bristly cheek. "Do you mean are you going to die?" He gave me a wry little smile. He shook his head. "I'm sorry things worked out this way, but you ought to do fine on chemotherapy. We'll hope so anyway." Then he looked directly at me in his nice way and said, "Betsy, I'm so sorry. I should never have gone along with this crazy scheme of yours. I feel responsible. Try to forgive me."

I actually managed to get to sleep that night—sleeping got me away from all this—but in the night I woke up and heard babies crying. For just a second I thought I was back in the women's hospital and then I remembered with a shock what had happened and had the vague thought that finally I was really crazy. But the next day I remembered that we were directly above the pediatrics ward and we could hear the kids whenever the windows were open, as they always were at night, winter and summer. I had never noticed before. And the worst of it was that when you have babies on your mind there seem to be babies everywhere. Someone gave me some ladies' magazines to look at to help fill the time—The Ladies Home Journal, McCalls and The Woman's Home Companion—but it seemed like there were babies on every page. I just put them on my stand and asked a nurse to take them back please. It was like the world was torturing me.

Early the next day the medical bureaucracy shifted into high gear and finally I was busy all morning long. It was actually a relief after so much time alone. I was still recovering from having had a baby so there were problems with that area that had to be dealt with. My breasts were full of milk and were really sore; every time I moved they leaked, so the front of my nightgown was soaking wet. My own OB wasn't about to come to see me, so one of the OB's from downstairs examined me and said I could have hardly any water to drink, they would give me dry-up pills and they would bind up my breasts. I got so preoccupied with how much that hurt that for a little while I managed not to think too much about the rest of it.

Every now and then Miss Ebersole came smiling in to my bare, lonesome room, obviously enjoying her victory. I don't remember if she actually said, "Now are you going to behave yourself?" but I got the message. She told me that she was shifting people around and would have me in with roommates soon. The way she said it didn't reassure me.

Finally, nearly twenty-four hours after the axe fell, they let Aunt Elfreda in to see me. I guess she stubbornly sat out in the waiting room until even Miss E. gave in. The lunch carts were just starting to rattle up the hall when her grey and life-worn face appeared in my doorway—or what I could see of it above the white mask. I burst out crying for the first time since they had first told me I had broken down.

She sat on my bed and held me in her arms and stroked my head and in her steadiest, strongest voice said, "There, there, my dear. These things happen. You'll be all right."

Aunt Elfreda had been to the women's hospital to see the baby that morning. She said the baby was fine and that the nurses really loved her and were being wonderful to her.

"They feel sorry for her, Betsy. There's someone in that little nursery with her all the time."

I asked Aunt Elfreda if they let her hold the baby, but she said no, she wasn't family, so they wouldn't allow it. But she told me that Mrs. Williams was going up that afternoon, and because she was the real grandmother maybe they would let her.

"Has Jimmy seen her?" Jimmy had never visited even once while I was in that other hospital.

"I don't think so." Aunt Elfreda said. "I wouldn't expect much from Jimmy."

So then my heart began to ache for my baby. I tried not to think about her because it seemed to me I truly, truly couldn't bear it, but I couldn't guard my thoughts every second, and talking like that let the longing flood in. I didn't want to sob again in front of Aunt Elfreda. After all, she wasn't ever going to see her little girl again; at least mine was still alive. But I couldn't help it, the tears just came and came no matter how hard I tried to shut them off.

While I cried, Aunt Elfreda went on calmly talking. She had seen the Williams the night before and they would take the baby to their house when the hospital finally released her. Polly Jo would be up to see me that afternoon and Mrs. Williams would come in the evening. Everyone sent their love. They would call my mother and tell her what had happened.

*   *   *   *

When Mrs. Williams didn't come and didn't come to see me I should have been suspicious, but I figured she was just busy getting ready to take care of the baby. But on the fourth day she suddenly appeared in the doorway of my room during afternoon visiting hours. She looked embarrassed and she didn't try to hug me or blow me a kiss or anything. I couldn't figure out what was wrong. Finally, without any warning, she said, "Betsy, Jimmy claims that she isn't his baby." She couldn't even look at me when she said it. "Could that be true?"

I couldn't believe my ears. That was my substitute mother, Mrs. Williams, saying such a ridiculous thing "I don't understand," I finally stammered. "Why would he have married me if he didn't believe he was the father? Whose else could it be? I didn't even know anyone else." I felt like someone had hit me.

"Apparently he went up to Pine Center and talked with your mother. He claims there is someone named Whitey in your life."

Now I really was crazy. Whitey? I hadn't seen Whitey since I was fourteen. I told Mrs. Williams that. I could tell that she didn't quite know whether to believe me.

"Your mother seemed very positive, according to Jimmy," she said.

"Mrs. Williams, my mother is crazy and is an alcoholic," I blurted out. All the time I had been trying to protect my mother, this was what I got for it.

"Betsy!" Mrs. Williams frowned at me. "Dear, you mustn't say such things."

I felt frantic. "No really, it's true. But why would Jimmy want to talk to her? What's going on?"

Mrs. Williams looked apologetic. "Now Betsy, try to understand. When we first learned of your pregnancy of course we all wanted to do the right thing. But Jimmy says now that he always doubted that he was the father. He tells us that you two were together only once and that he never believed he was responsible. Is that true?"

I was speechless. My stomach felt sick and my eyes felt blurry. The whole conversation was beginning to seem hazy and far away.

"We'll have to see what we're going to do," she went on, as if I had agreed. "Of course if it isn't our grandchild, it wouldn't be right for us to take it home." Then she stood up, patted my hand, and left.

All I could think was I have to talk to Dave, that he would know what to do, but then I couldn't think how to get in touch with him—he didn't come to see me regularly—so once again I was stuck and alone. But as things turned out,

Dave heard about it from Polly Jo that same afternoon. I guess she phoned him. Mrs. Williams couldn't have been gone for more than an hour when Dave came storming in. He was furious. He sat next to the bed and pounded both his fists on my bed covers.

"Those miserable, blankety blank people," he exploded. "All human kindness until their rotten, spoiled son has to take a little responsibility, and then they cave in like a bunch of marshmallows. Do you know that that creep told them they had to choose between him and your baby? If they took the baby, they could plan never to see him again."

Of course, I didn't know that. But I wasn't exactly surprised. "What should I do, Dave? What will happen to Melissa." I was numb. It all seemed to be out of my hands.

"I've contacted social service," Dave announced grimly. "It was the only thing to do. A social worker will be in to see you today. Maybe they can help you to work this thing out."

A social worker! My heart sank. Social workers were the ultimate bad news. It seemed to me that whenever any patient I had known got involved with a social worker, everything quickly went from bad to a whole lot worse. "I'm not talking to any social worker. No."

Dave looked me straight in the eye and let me have it. "Yes, you will. You have bullied me for the last time, lady. If you ever want to see that baby again you will talk to the social worker. Do I make myself clear?" It sounded tough but Dave's face was kind. Still, I wasn't feeling like trusting anybody, considering what had just happened.

"What will this person want? That's my baby. I don't need a social worker."

"Wrong on both counts," Dave noted bluntly. "And unless you want some bureaucratic know-it-all to decide it actually isn't your baby to keep, you need a social worker really badly"

So that scared me. Not enough to promise anything, but enough to talk to a social worker one time only. "Okay," I said reluctantly. "Just once. But don't expect much."

And then Dave abruptly left. I was afraid he was mad at me but I guessed maybe he was too upset to trust himself to say any more. And then, minutes later, I heard a tap on my open door and looked up to see a tall, thin, angular man in a surgical gown and mask, standing on one foot, leaning against the door frame. He had his other foot wrapped around his ankle and his arms crossed, a very picture of patience and relaxation. He was trying to look like this wasn't any big deal even though I would have been a fool not to realize that he and Dave were in cahoots.

"Hi," he said. "Are you Betsy?"

I said I was.

"I'm Don Bonner. I'm a social worker. Did the doctor tell you I might stop by?"

As if I didn't know. But I was surprised at his appearance. I had expected a woman and a not very nice woman at that. So this Don person threw me slightly off guard.

"Hello," I said, not very politely. "Come in. I guess I was expecting you. Sort of."

He straightened out his legs and ambled in, pulling down the mask so I could get a good look at his face. He had a sharp nose and thin lips in a small sidewise smile. He pulled the chair away from the bed and sat down. He stuck his legs out in front of him, put his hands behind his head, and looked out the window.

"I hear you've got some problems," he said casually.

I looked at him without his mask. "You're supposed to wear that thing you know."

He pulled it up over his mouth but not over his nose. "Okay," he said.

I wasn't in a mood for kidding around. "That won't do you any good. The germs can still get into your nose."

He widened his eyes and pretended to be surprised. "Really? Suppose I just breathe through my mouth?" He was teasing me.

It didn't help. I hunched myself up in bed, and then winced when my sore bottom and my sore front both hurt me at the same time. The social worker noticed my expression.

"Are you okay?" he asked. He seemed to be concerned, but then he would be, wouldn't he? "Is this a bad time to be here? I can come back later."

Still, something inside me didn't want him to go. I knew wasn't in a position to bargain with possible helpers, if that was what he really was.

"No, that's okay," I said reluctantly. "I'm just sore in a bunch of places. I'm fine." I was the teeniest bit touched that he should even care that I was hurting. Mostly hospital people ignored it.

"I had a long talk with your friend," he said, gesturing toward the door. "He told me about your baby. That's tough."

I embarrassed myself by starting to cry again. I shook my head helplessly at the social worker but I couldn't seem to stop.

"Hey," he said sympathetically. "I'd cry too. Go right ahead. I've got all the time in the world."

I sucked in my breath and held it. The tears kept right on running down my face. I looked apologetically at whatever-his-name was. "I'm sorry," I managed to say. "I'm not quite used to all this yet."

He waited for a few minutes till I calmed down and then he said, "Would it bother you too much to tell me what happened?" He glanced at me and then looked out the window again. "Let me tell you what I already know. Then you can fill in the details." He told me he knew about my medical history, about my leaving the hospital AMA (he smiled a little about that part), about Jimmy and the Williams, and about how I didn't know what was happening to Melissa. (It was amazing to me to hear someone else say her name. Made her sound like a person, not just a baby.) "Let's see," he said. "I can't remember details, but it seems to me that your mother is a problem too."

That was a funny way to put it. I actually smiled a little. "That's an under-statement." I leaned back and tried to explain about my mother. "She really is crazy," I said defiantly. "I know people don't believe that, but it's true. My brother told me all about it and he wouldn't lie to me."

"I believe you," the social worker said. "What about your brother? Is he around?"

That made me think about Joey and then I started to cry again. When I finally got control of myself, I waved my hand limply and said, "Boy, it doesn't take much!"

The social worker sat up and leaned forward. He pulled the chair over to my bed and rested his arms on it the way Dave had done. It was against every rule of isolation procedure in the book—you weren't ever supposed to touch a conta-gious patient's bed—but I decided not to tell him that; it seemed clear that he didn't care.

"You're worried about your brother," he observed.

Joey's thin, tired face popped into my mind and that didn't help the tears to stop. "He's the one who really needs a social worker," I whispered, catching my breath. "His life is a mess."

"Well, actually, we might be able to do something about that too," the social worker said mildly. "Who knows."

This conversation didn't seem to be going anywhere so I bit my lip and wiped my eyes and looked straight at whats-his-name. "Why are you here?" I asked him suspiciously. "What are you going to do?"

He didn't look away this time. I guess he decided to lay it on the line. "The doctor thought I could help you make plans for Melissa."

All the alarms in the world went off in my head. I sat bolt upright. That sneak! Pretending to be so friendly and nice when all the time he was there to get my baby.

"She's mine!" I said. "I won't give her up! I walked away from this place once. I'll do it again. You can't have her."

"Hey Betsy," the social worker said, hastily backing off. "Calm down. Of course she's yours. I'm not trying to get her away from you."

I didn't believe him. I told him so.

He sighed. "Okay, let me explain your legal rights to you. You can check them out with your doctor-friend—not that he'll know anything, but he can find out. Unless you've been neglectful, which you haven't, or abusive, which you haven't, nobody can take a mother's baby away from her without her permission."

I was doubtful. "So why do you hear all those stories about girls losing their kids?"

"Did you ever stop to wonder how you would explain it to people if you ever wanted to give a child away?"

"I wouldn't."

"I know, but sometimes mothers do. And the easiest way to keep people off their backs is to tell them that a social worker made them do it." He smiled a not very humorous smile. "Social work—the great unloved profession."

"So what are you telling me? That you're such a good guy you would never do that to me?"

"Sure," he said without smiling. "Considering everything, I don't know why you should believe me, but basically I'm telling you that I'm on your side and that no matter what you may think, I am here to help you keep Melissa and make plans for her. You know," he added, "that doctor is a good friend of yours. He thinks you're great."

I studied the social worker's bony, serious face. I felt as though I had to decide my whole future right then. I could trust him and maybe untangle the awful snarl that my life had gotten into, or I could be wrong and lose my baby and maybe ruin everything. He was slouched with his chin resting on the back of his hands and his nose about six inches away from my bed covers. Why would he take a silly chance like that if he didn't really want to help me?

"What did you say your name was?" I asked him.

He turned his head and looked quizzically at me. "Don," he said.

"Don what?"

"Don Bonner. Just call me Don."

"Well," I said reluctantly. "What should happen next? I'm not agreeing to anything, remember. She's mine. You can ask anyone around here; I don't give up easily. But go ahead and see what you can find out."

*   *   *   *

The social worker turned out to be a whirlwind once he got started. While I was being slowly processed through the cumbersome hospital system with tests and interviews with people from every department you can think of, Don apparently was off checking up on the corners of my other life. I started hearing about it first from visitors. Aunt Elfreda said he'd been to her house and they'd had a long talk. "A nice young man," was her approving comment. She wouldn't tell me what they talked about.

Then one day Polly Jo reported that she had met him for coffee in the hospital cafeteria on her way up to see me. Poor Polly Jo, she felt awful about what had happened with her family. She barged into my room without a mask or gown or anything. "So what," she said. "I'm going to catch TB?" When Miss Ebersole noticed her in with me and said sniffily that she should get gowned, Polly Jo said sweetly, "Okay," and then didn't budge. "It's the limp little kid approach," she told me cheerfully.

I wasn't sure what I should say to her about Melissa; would she believe that Jimmy wasn't the father? Of course I should have known better.

She sprawled on my bed—"no point in using my up-time," she observed—and tried to figure her brother out. "I don't know why my parents couldn't ever say no to him. He's your basic spoiled brat and always has been. I feel responsible, Bones. I told him what I thought in no uncertain terms, but it didn't do any good. He learned how to shut me out a long time ago. Now we aren't speaking, which is all right with me."

"What about your parents?"

"I just hope they'll come around. My mom thinks she can't stand to have Jimmy go away again; she just hated it when he was in Germany. My dad will mostly go along with my mom…you know how that goes."

"But you believe me that Jimmy is Melissa's father."

"Bones!" Polly Jo looked at me as though I was simple minded. "Who else? You haven't exactly been out on the town every night."

"What did the social worker say to you?"

Polly Jo was quiet for a minute. I could see she didn't know how much she ought repeat. "Bones, I think there is a little bit of a mess right now. He hasn't told you about it?" I told her she was scaring me. "I'm sorry. I'm sure everything will work out," she said, not very convincingly.

"Polly Jo! I can face up to anything if I have to. Remember? What do you mean by a mess?" I had a panicky moment thinking she might walk out without telling me.

"I'm not sure what it means exactly, but Melissa is in the hands of an adoption agency. Apparently the hospital asked them to get involved."

She reached over and squeezed one of my shoulders. "Take it easy, Bones. You can face anything, right? You've got this Don person working for you. You're going to have to trust him, I think."

"What do you mean she's in the hands of an adoption agency?" I had trouble choking out the words. I had a quick, sharp image of my soft, squirmy, sweet little baby.

Polly Jo stretched out across the foot of my bed and propped herself on an elbow. "Well the story as I understood it is that since the hospital couldn't send Melissa home to our house, they were stuck trying to figure out where she should go."

"Why don't they ask me?"

Polly Jo hesitated. "Bonesy, that OB who delivered her told them that he didn't think you would be able to take care of her."

I thought I couldn't breathe and that I was going to faint.

"Bones, are you okay?" Polly Jo sat up and looked at me. I shook my head no.

"Hang on!" she said as she slid off the bed. "Let me see if I can find Dave. He's here on the floor somewhere. We just were together." And she went racing out of the room.

After a minute Miss Ebersole appeared, looking rattled and confused. I was still trying to drag in my breath. Everything in my chest seemed to have shut down. Miss Ebersole propped me up into a sitting position and put her left hand on my diaphragm. "Now, now Betsy," she said tensely. "Just relax. We'll have you taken care of in a minute."

The room was starting to go around when Dave and Polly Jo came back. Dave shoved Miss E. aside and I felt a needle in my arm. After a few seconds, my chest loosened up and I started to get my breath. When I finally got some air and my head cleared, I noticed that Miss Ebersole was gone. Dave was standing beside me with one hand on my pulse and the other on my head. Polly Jo was on the other side looking scared.

"Feeling better?" Dave said as he let his hand slide onto my shoulder. I nodded. "Sit down, P.J. Let's the three of us have a little chat. Who's going to tell me what happened just now?"

Polly Jo gave me a tentative glance and, when I nodded, she told Dave what she had told me. The words didn't sound quite so terrifying a second time, but I still had to concentrate on relaxing and I didn't think I should risk talking.

Dave frowned. He put his fingers together and cracked his knuckles. He swore some, then he apologized to me for his language.

"Let's find that social worker," he said. "I want to know all the details. Betsy, you were right about that OB apparently. I never learn, do I? You seem to be right about a lot of things." He got up. "I'll be back," he said. "Maybe the guy's still in the building." He went off on a half run and only a few minutes later was back. "He'll be right up," Dave reported. "I caught him in his office, so that's a break."

Don, the social worker, wasn't so relaxed and casual this time. He was still pulling on a gown as he came through my door, and he didn't even have a mask in his hand. He gave a little wave to Polly Jo and shook hands with Dave. He started to talk while standing by the foot of the bed, but Polly Jo jumped up and offered him her chair. "I'll sit on the bed," she said as she climbed up and sat there with her legs crossed. I was sitting the same way at the other end of the bed. We both looked expectantly at Don.

"She's pretty upset." Dave told him. "Maybe you'd better explain what's going on. What's this business with her OB?"

Don rubbed his face with both hands and then ran them through his hair. "Oh lord," he said wearily. "I should have come up and told you right away. I knew you'd be upset but I thought I could get some other wheels in motion before I had to tell you."

Dave looked stern. "I think Betsy could handle this better if she knew all the facts."

"I suppose so," Don said apologetically. "Let me repeat to her and to you what I said the other day. That obstetrician is full of…well you know what he's full of. Unless Betsy is abusive or neglectful, nobody…" he looked at me hard…"Nobody can take her baby away from her. Do you hear me Betsy?" I shrugged. "Okay, you don't have to believe me. I'll bring copies of the law and I'll let you talk to an attorney, okay?"

Dave was still frowning. "Why is the women's hospital doing what they're doing?"

Don crossed his arms and settled back in his chair. "Let me see if I can explain. It isn't as bad as it sounds." He leaned forward and stared me straight in the face. "It's not as bad as it sounds," he repeated firmly. He continued to look at me flat-out until he wheedled a little smile out of me.

"Okay," he said. "That's better. I talked to the head nurse and to their social worker. They have to discharge Melissa in the next couple of days and because of the questions Betsy's doctor raised, they felt they needed the judgment of an out-side agency about where she should go. I told them all about Mrs. Boyle and about Betsy's family and they will be sending someone up here to talk to her." Don's remarks were mostly addressed to Dave.

"Don't talk to Dave, talk to me," I said. "She's my baby, not Dave's."

Don shifted his attention to me. "Sorry," he said. "What do you want to know?"

"I want to know why Aunt Elfreda can't take her home. That's where I want her to go."

Don hesitated. "Betsy, I gather that your aunt also has a history of TB."

"How did you know that?"

"Well, she told me so, but more importantly, she told your obstetrician."

"Why would she have done that?"

"I gather they got into an argument about your future. That idiot has a thing about tuberculosis. If I'm feeling charitable I could say it's because he is an old man with old fashioned ideas. One of them is that TB is the white plague and once you have it you can kiss a normal life goodbye."

"You don't believe that, do you?" I asked.

"No of course not. Would I be sitting here soaking up your germs if I believed that?" He tried out another experimental smile on me. I didn't bite.

"Anyway," he went on, "he's told that other hospital that he will raise the issue to the juvenile court if the hospital tries to send Melissa to your aunt's." He watched me to see if I was getting upset.

Dave broke in. "He's a miserable sanctimonious know-it-all. I thought so while Betsy was pregnant and he would send me little holier-than-thou reports. He patted me on the head by mail, if that's possible."

"Yeah, I know what you mean," Don said. "I had to keep a tight lid on my temper when I talked to him."

"You talked to him?" I said. "What did you tell him?"

"I told him I was representing your interests, that I had no reason to think that Mrs. Boyle couldn't care for Melissa, and that if he wanted a court hearing I would guarantee that he would find he didn't have a case."

"Doesn't sound like you kept too tight a lid on your temper," Dave observed with a slight smile.

"Oh yeah. I was just as cool as I could be. Let the bastard take it to court. He doesn't have a leg to stand on."

"I don't understand why he goes to all this bother," Polly Jo put in.

Don looked reflective. "Some day I'm going to write a book about doctors' irrational prejudices. It's part of the God syndrome."

I said I didn't understand.

Dave explained. "He's right. You handle life and death decisions every day for years and it becomes hard to remember that you don't necessarily have all the answers to everything. I have trouble with that myself sometimes."

"So what happens next?" I asked again, more crossly this time, directing the question at Don.

He thought for a minute. "Well," he said slowly, "I suppose we need to see how to get your aunt approved to take care of Melissa. Betsy, that may mean talking to an agency person. I think I'd better warn you so you won't be upset when someone appears at your door."

I was on guard again. I was getting tired of that tight throat feeling. "What would they want from me? Why can't I just say where I want Melissa to go?"

"It would be a precaution. If they've studied Mrs. Boyle's situation and have a signed statement from you, it would be very hard for either the other doctor or," he looked warily at Polly Jo, "the Williams to object."

Polly Jo frowned. "Nobody's going to object," she observed. "I think my mom is just as embarrassed as she can be by what she's done. She'll be glad to know the baby is with Mrs. Boyle."

Dave had been listening carefully. "Betsy, do you feel okay about this? Is there anything we're missing?"

I thought about my own family. "Could I call my brother?" I asked. "He'd want to know what's happening. And I'd like my aunt Janine to know too."

"You bet," Dave said. "Right now. I'll get a stretcher."

So I climbed onto a wheeled stretcher and tied a mask over my face. As we went by, Miss Ebersole appeared out of the nurses' station and started to say something, but when she saw Dave she didn't dare. He rolled me down to the pay phone at the end of the hall and dialed the number for me.

Joey answered the phone. He sounded sleepy. I said who it was and he said he couldn't understand me. I looked at Dave and pointed to my mask. Miss Ebersole was watching us from up the hall but Dave just stared back at her as he untied my mask and took it off.

I tried talking into the phone again. "Joey, it's me. Can you understand me now?" He said he could. "Listen," I said as firmly as I could, "I have to see you. It's really important."

He asked me why; Joey never did use very many words for things.

"I'm back in the hospital, Joey," I said. "I'm basically okay, but an awful lot has happened that I need to tell you about and I can't tell you over the phone. Please, could you come to see me soon?"

I didn't hear anything for a minute and then I heard him clear his throat. "Um, let's see," the low, tired voice said. "I suppose I can come after work tomorrow. How'll I find you?"

I looked at Dave. I remembered that Joey had never even once been to the hospital. I thought, Well even though he sounds bored with me, really he is probably feeling scared and wondering what's going on. I put my hand over the phone so Joey couldn't hear.

"Get Polly Jo, will you?" I asked Dave.

He nodded and walked casually but fast back toward my room—no sense in getting Miss E. stirred up again. In a minute he and Polly Jo were doing the same thing back in the other direction. I chit-chatted a little bit with Joey while I waited, and then explained that I had to talk to a friend for a minute.

I put my hand over the mouthpiece. "Polly Jo," I asked her," could you meet my brother by the front door of the hospital tomorrow morning? He's coming down to see me and I think he's scared of this place."

As I said it, I realized that, of course, that must be a big reason why he'd never been to see me.

Polly Jo nodded "sure" and I went back to the phone call. I explained to Joey what was going to happen. I could tell by his tone of voice that that was a load off his mind, but of course he said it wasn't necessary.

On an impulse, I handed the phone to Polly Jo, who said, "Hi Joe, this is Polly. Hey, don't hurt my feelings. I want to meet you, hear? Anyway, how'd I feel if you got lost in this big ole place? I can show you around and give you a really good time." Polly Jo lowered her voice with that last sentence and kind of growled it. Then she handed me back the phone.

I heard Joey laugh and I thought to myself, well you never know when a small idea will turn out to be a good one.

CHAPTER 6

▼

NEW FRIENDS

For once Miss Ebersole wasn't as mean as I had remembered. On the sixth day after I was back on the floor, a couple of orderlies came in and announced they were moving me. By then I wouldn't much have cared where they took me I was so sick of being by myself. I had begun to string out conversations with cleaning women and lab technicians and anybody else who came into my room, just to have someone to talk to. I started worrying that I was getting a reputation as a gabber and people would start avoiding me. So when my bed with me in it, and a stretcher full of my possessions, were wheeled into a big four bed ward near the nurses station, and I saw my old friend Marcella, who'd spent all those years on the Stryker frame, sitting in a chair, I was so glad to see her I was almost light hearted for the first time since before Melissa was born.

"The prodigal returns," Marcella said with a big smile, as my bed was pushed into an empty place by the door. "Sorry, I can't get up to greet you, but as you can see, this is an improvement over the last time you saw me. There's hope for the future."

I just stared and stared at Marcella. When she was lying on her frame she had looked puffy and sort of like a blob. Every few hours someone would sandwich her between two stretcher-like boards and with a big crank would flop her over onto her back or onto her stomach, depending on which side she needed to have down. When she was on her stomach, her forehead would rest at the edge of a hole that her face could poke through, and her arms would hang down so she could feed herself or write letters or whatever. Otherwise she wasn't supposed to move. When she was on her back she just stared at the ceiling. We always wondered how she could stand it.

But sitting up like that, I could see that while she was big and heavy, she had shoulders and breasts and hips and long, skinny legs with no muscles on them, and a wide, pale face with prominent cheek bones and a big mouth. I had never had a good look at her face before. Someone had cut her mousy hair into bangs and a straight bob—it wasn't very becoming, but at least she was trying to fix herself up. When she grinned I could see gaps in her teeth. She would never tell us how old she was but we always thought she must be fairly old because she had been there for so long.

I just grinned back at her. It was like I had never been away except that now this wonderful thing had happened. "Wow, Marcella, look at you! You look great. Polly told me you were off the frame, but I didn't know you were getting up. That's wonderful."

"Miracle drugs, kid," Marcella informed me. "They always said just be patient and maybe we'll find a cure, but who ever thought they'd really do it."

She stood up and I was amazed by how tall she was. As tall as any man. "Time to get back to bed," she said as she positioned herself carefully on the edge of her bed and swung her legs up. "Careful, careful; don't want to jar anything loose." She winced a little as she settled herself flat on her back and pushed her pillow under her head. "The old bod is a little stiff," she observed.

The orderly pushed my bed into a corner near the sink. I looked around. Nothing had changed. Same old iron beds, same old tan metal bed stands, same old lockers near the door, same old cracked ceiling. But there was one huge difference. Backed up to the windows and facing the four beds was a big television set.

I had only seen one other TV before, in a motel room where I stayed once when I went to see Joey. You put a quarter in a slot in the top and got a teeny little moving picture for exactly twenty five minutes, which meant that if it was a thirty minute show you had to put in another quarter. It had never occurred to me that I would be in a hospital room with a TV. A big TV.

Marcella saw me staring at it and said, "Ruthie's got pull. And money. You can thank her for the TV."

I looked around to see who she meant and a spare, dark haired woman, maybe forty or so, waved at me from across the room, in the bed by the left window.

"Ruth Evans, meet Betsy," said Marcella.

Then I noticed in the other inside bed, directly across from me, was a young pointy faced girl with long, straight brown hair. "Hi, Betsy," she said softly, acknowledging my glance. "I'm Eleanor Rugerowski."

I noticed that Eleanor looked awfully serious, even kind of sad. But Ruth looked nice and as if she would be easy to talk to. Her night stands were neat and had little bouquets of flowers on them. I could see framed pictures of older kids and it occurred to me that it would be nice to room with another mother.

It turned out that a few other things had changed for the better. For instance, we now could have visitors twice a day. Time rolled itself backward, and the year and a half outside was a dream that happened to someone else.

The nurses were mostly the same; Miss Maple, the night nurse, answered my light the first night I was back and didn't even acknowledged that I'd been gone. "Do you want a bedpan, Betsy?" she said in that dry, nighttime voice, and then she brought it, and then came back and got it, and never turned on the light or asked me how I was or told me what a terrible thing I had done or anything. Amazing.

The only nurse who talked to me about it was one that we called Charlie. Her name was Miss Charles, but she was such a character you couldn't think of her as Miss anything. She always walked around slowly, looking like she'd been drugged. We wondered how she ever found the energy to do the work, but in fact she was a pretty good nurse. Polly Jo used to say she operated on two cylinders and rusty spare parts, but if you didn't drive her up too many hills she ran okay.

The next morning Charlie was assigned to give me one of her typical, sloppy bed-baths—she always managed to get the bed pad wet, so when she changed the sheets, you were still lying in a wet bed. She surprised me by asking me, in a really kind voice, what had happened to me.

"I worried about you, you know," she said. "I'm sorry you had to come back. I hear that you have a baby. Is she okay?"

So that gave me a chance to tell Charlie my story, which was a help, and after that Charlie would always ask me how Melissa was and how I was feeling about things. I don't even think she wrote it down on my chart.

My new roommates, on the other hand, wanted to know all the details about everything. I can't begin to explain how wonderful it was to be with people again. That first night we laid awake and talked and talked. I learned that Eleanor's husband had left her after she got sick, and that her mother had her two kids, who she hadn't seen for six months. She felt so awful about them that she didn't even have any pictures taped to her reading rack or her tray table the way the rest of us did. I hadn't ever known a really depressed person before Eleanor. We all worried about her.

Ruth was a doctor and she thought she had caught TB from her patients. She was allergic to streptomycin so she was taking what she called an old fashioned cure. She was cheery and matter of fact during the day, but we could hear her crying at night. Still, her husband was a great guy; he came every day, and sometimes on Sundays she would get in a wheelchair and he would sneak her downstairs to see her children. That was against the rules in a lot of ways, but I guess she had pull with somebody. It was interesting rooming with a doctor, and Ruth could explain lots of things to us that we wouldn't otherwise have known. Sometimes we got special treatment because of her, like extra food, or better stands by our beds, or even an electric floor fan when the weather got hot. Also, Miss Ebersole had trouble being gruff with Ruth. She just naturally got sappy around doctors and a lady doctor in bed didn't change that.

During the time I was out in the world all the patients, not just the really sick ones, had started receiving streptomycin and another drug that we called P.A.S. I learned that patients got shots in their bottoms three times a week. Supposedly they didn't hurt you, but sometimes the shots made it hard to lie on that side—I guess I had some kind of skin reaction. Also the shots made me light headed and as if I had pins and needles in my lips and fingers. The docs said don't worry about it, but I worried anyway, but it was a lot better than having surgery, I can tell you that. The P.A.S. was enormous pills which we took six at a time, four times a day. Followed by an antacid! I got so I could put that pile of horse pills in my right hand, throw them in my mouth, and wash them all down with one gulp of water. Nothing to it.

Because of the drugs, a lot of the surgery had stopped. There were no more pneumos, so that was good, and no more thoracoplasties, which was even better. Instead, the surgeons kept busy with something called "resections." I heard it explained that they peeled away sections of your lung just like sectioning an orange. Because I had disease on both sides, they didn't want to do that to me, but they had their eye on Eleanor, and finally they took her away. We never saw her again because after surgery the word was that she had a nervous breakdown and they sent her to the state hospital. I asked Don about it and he said he couldn't tell us much but that he was following her case and he understood that they were trying one of the new nerve drugs on her. That's all we ever knew.

*   *   *   *

Joey was different when he was away from Mom. He came to see me that first time dressed in a blue suit and a red tie and I felt proud of him. Of course he was still serious, but he didn't seem as scared as I would have thought. Polly Jo seemed different too, more grown up and thoughtful. I could see that she was impressed by my brother.

"You never told me he was so good looking," she later said to me.

I told her sarcastically that I thought she was spoken for, so that caused a little chilliness between us for a while.

Joey took his cues from Polly Jo about how to behave as a visitor, and Polly Jo put on her best visitor's act. She sat three feet from my bed in a straight chair, and she didn't touch anything, and she made polite small talk with Marcella and Ruth. Why we didn't all break out in giggles is still a wonder, but everyone was hoping that Joey would have a nice time so he would want to come back.

He came by himself a couple of times after that—or rather, Polly Jo brought him a couple of times—but one day he showed up with someone else; a bony kid, all elbows and knees and nervous energy. I knew him right away!

Whereas Joey had changed a lot in five years, my brother Tony was just a jumbo size version of himself as a kid. No blue suit on him; he had been slicked into clean jeans and an almost clean t-shirt, but even Aunt Janine hadn't been able to get real leather shoes on him, and when he awkwardly crossed his legs I noticed he wasn't wearing socks. But then, he was still a teenager in every way, including being so self-conscious I'm sure he would have dived through the window to get out if he had had to stay longer than half an hour. Poor Tony—he couldn't even pretend he wasn't nervous and scared and only Joey doing a big brother routine held him in that chair for a respectable length of time.

I didn't feel related to him, isn't that odd? He belonged to Aunt Janine now. I didn't have to worry about him or take responsibility for him and he was obviously not feeling connected to me, or Joey either, so inside of myself I let him go. I guess for all those years there had been a walled off sore place that was my habit of taking care of Tony, and now I could let it heal. After they left I noticed that I felt looser. And to think I had never even noticed that that was bothering me.

*   *   *   *

Melissa was nearly three weeks old when she finally went to Aunt Elfreda's. The agency lady who came to see me tried to be nice, but I could tell she was suspicious of me.

When I told Don that, he sucked in his cheeks and made a long face and pretended to be writing on a yellow pad the way she had done.

"I know this must be hard for you, Miss," he said mockingly, stressing that last word, "but do you mind if I ask you a few questions?" Then his teeth smiled at me while he squinted his eyes.

I couldn't help laughing, even though she hadn't been the least bit funny at the time. She had long dark hair in a pageboy curl, and even though she must have been at least forty she looked as if she was still pretending to be a girl. Her voice was very soft and girly too; sometimes I couldn't make out what she was saying. She sounded reassuring, even when she was saying things like, "What were you feeling when you walked out of the hospital two years ago?"

How could I explain what I was feeling without sounding like an irrational loony? We played an unreal little game. She tried to make her questions sound like she didn't think I was impulsive, immature, and irresponsible, and I tried to make my answers sound like I was being honest, open and cooperative.

She must have had to clear her visits with Don's office, because thirty seconds after she left the floor, he appeared; just before I dissolved into hysterical babbling. The first time she came he was a few minutes late and through my tears I could see Marcella and Ruthie waving their hands toward me as if to say "do something!"

He marched over to my bed, pulled the white privacy curtain all the way around on the overhead track and then, against all the rules in the universe, sat on my bed and put his arms around me. He hugged me so tight I couldn't tremble enough to be hysterical, and then when I had calmed down a little bit he tickled me in the ribs.

"Don't do that!" I gasped, trying not to laugh.

"Why not?" he said, doing it again.

"Because this is serious!" I said, trying to sound angry.

"I know it," he said, squeezing me until my breath came out in a little puff of air and then letting me go. He put his sharp nose against the end of mine and stared into my eyes. "Gee you have blue eyes," he said, irrelevantly.

"Don, you'll catch something," I said, putting a hand over my mouth and trying to push him away with my other hand. He let go of me and lounged across my legs, propping his chin in his hand.

"I gather you had a pleasant visit with Miss Know-It-All," he remarked with a smile.

"Don, you are still on my bed. I can't talk until you're sitting in a chair."

Seven years of conditioning wasn't to be wiped out by one minor episode of hysteria. Anyway, I had the thought that if Miss Ebersole were ever to hear about it, not only would Don instantly be sent wherever naughty social workers go—to the venereal disease unit probably—I would finally once and for all be packaged up and tagged incorrigible and sent to join poor Eleanor wherever she finally ended up.

I kicked Don. "Off!" I repeated.

He grinned at me and slid smoothly into the chair.

"Don, don't kid around anymore. That woman was awful. I'm scared."

He pretended to ignore me. "My feelings are hurt because I promised you on my word of honor that nothing bad was going to happen to Melissa and you don't believe me."

If I could have reached him, I would have hit him.

"Don't you dare play big daddy with me. You can't promise something like that because you don't know what's going to happen."

Suddenly the expression on Don's face changed. He stared at me and then sat up straight in the chair. I had never seen him look so intense. I guess I must have stared too, because after a minute he reached out his hands to me, and when I took them, he said seriously, "Betsy may I ask you a really hard question?"

I had no idea what was coming, but Don's hands were strong and warm and I realized again that I trusted him. "Okay," I said.

"Where's your dad?"

Well I hadn't expected that one.

I tried to think about my dad. It was as if he was very, very small, a miniature person in a miniature memory in a faded landscape, far, far away. I closed my eyes. In my mind's eye I could see his back walking away from me down the front walk of the house in Pine Center. He turned and waved, and I waved back. I don't think I was sad. I expected him to come back apparently, but he never did.

"I don't know where he is. He left us when I was seven."

"You've never heard from him? Is he alive?"

"I don't know."

"Does your mother talk about him?"

"Nobody pays any attention to my mother."

"What does she say about him?"

What did my mother say about him? My mind froze. I knew she said lots of things but they wouldn't come back to me. The harder I tried to remember the more confused I felt. I looked at Don and for a minute I couldn't think who he was. I looked around the big bare room. Where was I? My thoughts had stopped.

Don let me alone for a little while but then I guess he realized I was in trouble. "Betsy?"

"Betsy I want you to look at me," he said earnestly, hunching his chair close to my bed. "It's Don, sweetheart. Remember me?"

He took my hand and held it up to his face. I felt his stubbly chin and his cool cheeks. I moved my hand up into his thin hair and around his small flat ears. When I started to pull it away, he took it in his own again and kissed the palm. "Are you back?" he asked.

I looked at him and his face was an anchor in the present time. "Don, I forgot where I was. I'm in the hospital aren't I? I can't think how old I am."

"You're twenty years old. You are the mother of a baby girl named Melissa. You have TB but you're taking streptomycin and you're getting well. You have an adopted aunt who loves you and who is going to take care of Melissa. You were trying to remember your father but memories of your mother got in the way. Apparently your father made promises to you which he couldn't keep, so when I just made you a promise you felt like a little child again."

Don's hands were tightly squeezing mine as he said those things, and I felt held by his green eyes which never left my face.

"Are you hearing me? I want you to talk to me, Betsy. Say whatever is in your mind, no matter how foolish it feels."

Suddenly, suddenly I was seven again. I remembered screaming "I want my daddy," and my mother's hand over my mouth until I couldn't breathe. I remembered her saying "If you don't shut up right now Missy, I'll make you so sorry you'll never forget it." When did that happen? It seemed as though I was hearing a phone ring. Did I answer it? Was that Daddy's voice? It was too vague. I just remembered the sensation of being smothered by my mother's hand and that threat, always and forever associated with not breathing.

"Can you talk about it?" Don asked.

I shook my head no.

"Try, Betsy. You remembered your father. Tell me what you remembered."

"I'm afraid."

"You're afraid of your mother, Betsy. But she can't hurt you now. You're not a little girl anymore. You're grownup and smart and strong." Don grinned at me. "You once escaped from this place, remember? You can do anything you set your mind to do, can't you?"

Then the connection came to me. "If I tell you, they'll take Melissa."

"If you tell me about your father, your mother will take Melissa and you'll never see her again? The way you never saw your father again?

I felt my breath start to drag the way it had before.

"I can't breathe again, Don."

But in an instant Don was on the bed stretched out beside me with his arms around me so that as his chest breathed in and out it pressed against me. His cheek was against mine and his voice sounded in my ear.

"Just relax, sweetheart. Let's breathe together. In and out. In and out. See it's easier already. In and out. In and out."

I felt his warm breath on my face when he exhaled. After a few minutes I felt limp and tired.

He put an arm under my head and rolled onto his back beside me.

"I'm right here," he said. "Now I want you to talk about your father."

CHAPTER 7

▼

THE KIDNAPPING

Aunt Elfreda started bringing in pictures of Melissa, who was smiling now and starting to eat fruit and cereal and was looking more and more like Jimmy, which Aunt Elfreda couldn't resist pointing out to anyone who would listen.

"Isn't she adorable. Looks just like her daddy."

She and I both thought that was funny, though why we assumed the Williams wouldn't zoom back onto the scene with big grandparent nets I'm not sure. We just figured they'd had their chance, and anyway, by then I thought Don was God and could do anything as far as Melissa's welfare was concerned.

Another thing that was making me cocky was the obvious, goo goo eyed romance between Polly Jo and my brother. To all of our surprise, big smart Dave had been crowded off the court by an unassuming factory worker from up-state. Even more to our surprise, Dave was a bad sport about it. Even though he and his family were back together, he couldn't resist hanging around when he thought Polly Jo would be seeing me, and he tried to find out all about Joey, which wasn't much because I wasn't going to tell him much. But apparently he tried to explain to Polly Jo that she could "do better" which was certainly the wrong tactic, considering her stubborn streak. So old Dave had another broken heart. Some people never learn.

Joey was like a new person. He developed a little skipping walk; I could always tell his footsteps in the hall. And he thought everything Polly Jo said was funny; I'm sure he made up for a lifetime of not laughing in the first few months he knew her. But wonder of wonders, she turned out to have a streak of her mother in her a mile wide. She cooked and sewed and fussed and gave advice till any other mortal man would have been driven to shelter screaming for relief from smothering. But Joey was like a cat who had just learned about being scratched; he would turn himself around and around and figuratively rub against her legs and purr so loud everybody in the world could hear him.

At first he just came down to see her on his nights off, but pretty soon days and nights started running into each other and he sometimes used the "Betsy-cot" at the Williamses. Then he and our mom had a row which ended up with Mom throwing all the furniture from his bedroom out the window into the street. That time Joey got tough and told the state hospital he didn't care what they did with her but he wasn't taking care of her any more. Aunt Janine then invited him and Polly Jo over for Sunday dinner and sent me a really nice letter saying she was sorry I couldn't be there too, and that she would be up to see me as soon as she could make it.

Funny the way things work out. As Joey slid in, Jimmy slid out. Since his not being Melissa's father was not a story even his mother could buy anymore, he decided to make his fortune in California and with some elaborate story about the new plastics industry there, he cashed his veteran's bonus, bought another new car, and headed west. Mrs. Williams never apologized to me or to Aunt Elfreda. But she started buying little things for Melissa, and pretty soon started referring to herself as Grandma, which bothered Aunt Elfreda for a while, till I suggested that she could be "Nana" which had a more old fashioned flavor to it.

Finally Mrs. Williams had come up to see me at the hospital. "Just like old times," she said. At that point I decided Joey and I needed all the mothers we could get, so I never let on that anything bad had happened between us.

*   *   *   *

One afternoon after all the visitors had left, Marcella, Ruth and I were playing a quiet game of bridge while we waited for the supper carts. Marcella used her up-time to carry our hands to us in our beds. We played with five decks of cards so we could deal each person five hands at a time, then we would all agree to play a game with, say, the blue cards, and then bid for the dummy each time. Marcella was a phenomenal bridge player; Ruthie and I learned a lot from her. But this afternoon I was winning and it was making me feel cocky and optimistic.

During this bridge game, Ruth apparently decided to take advantage of my good humor. "Bets," she asked. "Did you ever fall in love with one of your doctors the way P.J. did with Dave?"

Since I hadn't ever thought of the Polly Jo/Dave affair as "falling in love with your doctor," I wasn't quite sure how to answer. Falling in love with a set of eyes above a surgical mask stretches even a young girl's imagination—eyes and a voice and what you can see of a body under a loose white gown—but I had had regular crushes on various residents over the years.

"I suppose so," I told her.

"Why do you suppose that was so? You didn't really know them, after all."

I wasn't quite sure what Ruth was driving at. "I don't know. Why do kids fall in love with movie stars? Same thing isn't it?"

"Why is it the same thing?"

"Well, you can imagine them to be anything you want, since you don't really know them."

"And doctors are extra nice to you so you can imagine that they feel something special for you?"

"I suppose so. Don't doctors ever feel special about certain patients?"

"Oh sure they do. Of course. Gosh, we're human too. But Betsy, we try to be very careful to draw a line between personal and professional behavior."

Usually I was pretty quick at getting the point of Ruthie's object lessons, but this time she lost me.

"Do I know a doctor besides Dave, who certainly doesn't count, who is unprofessional?"

"Maybe not a doctor…." she left the sentence dangling.

The light dawned. "Are you asking me if there is something going on between Don and me?" I laughed out loud. "He's just Don. I know he does just awful, crazy things, but that's why he's so wonderful."

"Awful crazy things like pulling your curtain and lying on your bed?"

"He only did that once. He saved my life, Ruthie."

Ruth sighed. "You know, it's funny. I think that is literally true. Did you know that we could hear most of what you were saying that day?"

"About my father?"

"Yes, I'm sorry. It was impossible not to listen, wasn't it Marcella?" Ruth looked over at Marcella who was squashed into a wooden arm chair trying to look disinterested.

"Sorry kid," Marcella said to me. "My parents weren't great either, but I wouldn't want the whole world to know about it. We've never talked about it, you know. Not even to each other. In fact," she glanced at Ruth, "I'm not quite sure why doctor smarty-pants is making a big deal of it now."

"Betsy, I'm going to give you a little lecture, okay? I don't do this to you very often, do I?"

I studied Ruth. She didn't look very doctorish in her pink bed jacket and her braided hair. She reached over to her stand and put her gold rimmed glasses on her nose, which made her look more serious, and then she picked up her knitting so she wouldn't have to look at me.

"Betsy, when you study psychology as you are going to do when you go to college (Ruthie was convinced I was going to college, even though I had hardly even been to high school) you will learn about something called Transference."

She put down her knitting, picked up a pad and pencil and wrote the word in big capital letters so that I could easily see it across the room.

"See? Well transference means taking strong feelings you had about your parents when you were a little child, either good feelings or bad feelings, and attaching them to other adults later on, adults who may or may not at all resemble those parents you are still remembering from long ago. When adults take care of us, the way medical people do, it is almost impossible not to cast some of them in the role of parents, whether we mean to or not. And since little children are really in love with their opposite-sex parent, they can really fall in love with opposite-sex, care-taking persons." She stopped and looked up.

I was puzzled. "Why didn't I fall in love with Dave, then?"

"Dave was very professional with you. He didn't flirt with you and he only touched you when there was a reason for it."

"Dave flirted with everybody."

"Not really. Dave was…is…very up-front with everybody, but he is very skillful at knowing where to draw the lines."

"You mean he was out to get Polly Jo."

"There's no doubt in my mind about that."

"Do men fall in love with their nurses?"

"You know they do."

"What does this have to do with Don. I'm not in love with Don. He's wonderful and he's the best social worker in the whole world, but I'm not in love with him." I could feel my neck getting hot as I said that, and I hoped I was far enough away so it didn't show.

Marcella's up-time was over and as she heaved herself onto her bed she said casually, "I wonder how many patients Don gets into bed with."

Now I was getting mad. "That's a dirty thing to say! I don't want to talk about this any more, and if I didn't trust you both never, never to tell anybody what you know I'd be really upset."

Ruth sighed. "Okay honey, I'm sorry. I like Don too, but I do think he is a little loose with common sense. I just want to be sure that you recognize that he can make mistakes too, and that you don't in fact, know much about him."

So, forewarned, I approached Don head-on the next time he drifted in during some illegal hour when he had manufactured a thin, fanciful excuse for needing to talk to me. He always carried a clipboard and my file with the name written in big letters.

"See," he would say to Miss Ebersole. "Business."

As usual, he pulled his chair right up to my bed and leaned his chin on his crossed arms. I realized that usually I slid way down when I talked to him so that our faces weren't very far apart and (or so I thought) we couldn't be overheard. I liked to talk to Don about everything—I would save up subjects—once I told him I needed to keep a list so I wouldn't forget anything. He would string a mask around his neck and if we heard footsteps in the hall, he could quickly pull it over his face and loop the tied ends around his ears. My bed was behind the door, so it was hard to sneak up on me.

"Don," I said softly to him one day. "Ruthie says I don't know very much about you. She's afraid I'm going to have a transference and get into trouble with you."

Don looked at me as if he hadn't quite heard me right, and then pushed back his chair and started to laugh.

"Have a transference, eh?" he said loudly. "The worst thing. Mostly fatal. But luckily in school I learned all kinds of ways of modifying and softening transference. Only doctors are allowed to cure transference of course, so the rest of us have to be very, very careful."

All that was directed at Ruth, who slid her glasses down her nose and stuck out her tongue at him. He returned the compliment and then pulled back up close to me.

"What do you want to know, sweetie? Ruth is right. It would be better if you knew as much about me as I know about you. Then you couldn't imagine me to be superman."

"Super-dad."

"Hey, you got it. Shall we start with my faults and failures?"

"Do you have some?" I was only half kidding.

"Oh lordy, a case of transference already is in progress. I could bring in my personnel file; that would give you a small picture of some of my less skillful indiscretions. That business with Sanctimonious Suzy from the adoption agency elicited a fairly nasty letter which is now in my file."

"Really?" I was amazed. "What did you do?"

"I kidnapped Melissa."

"Don! You never told me that."

"See, now I'm going to be unprofessional and indiscrete again. Promise me you won't have another one of your infamous asthma attacks." He smiled sweetly at me and batted his eyes.

"You *are* a flirt. Ruthie was right."

"I am a notorious flirt," he said loudly again. "Ruth is always right."

Ruthie replied this time. "If you are really going to have true confessions over there, pull that privacy curtain."

Don got up and walked over to Ruth's bed. He leaned over and kissed her on the forehead. Then he came back and pulled my curtain around us, so that we were in a tiny, round, white world.

"Bear in mind that I can still see your feet," Ruthie warned from the other side.

"How are you going to explain this curtain to Big Nurse when she comes snooping by?" he called back.

Marcella answered. "Betsy has a bed-pan, dumb-head. Just be sure you do lift up your feet if that happens."

This time Don stretched out an arm to me and I rested my cheek on the palm of his hand. We were whispering.

"What do you mean, you kidnapped Melissa?"

"She was in a foster home. The hospital knew they'd never get paid if they kept her, since there was nothing wrong with her medically, so while the agency was doing its big home study, they kept her in one of their storage places."

"Oh Don." I felt my eyes fill up.

"Uh-uh," he said, cupping my face with his free hand. "She was fine. The foster mother was terrific, in fact. Had taken care of so many babies she was a real pro. Did a lot better job than any of us could have done. But when I found out Melissa wasn't in the hospital any more..."

"How'd you find that out?"

"Sweetie, I went up to see her every day. I told you that."

I didn't remember, but then, there were a lot of things I had mercifully forgotten.

"Anyway, I arrived at the nursery and no Melissa. The head nurse and I were buddies by then, so she told me that the agency had taken her."

"How could they do that without telling me?"

"A gooood question! Old kindly Dr. Scrooge got into the act and ordered her discharged, I guess. If you ever have several hundred thousand spare bucks I would suggest that you sue him."

"How did you find her?"

"I'm not charming and devious for nothing," Don whispered, giving me a small smile. "I connived with *our* hospital social service department—our secretary to be exact—to call their nursery and say that it was important for our records department to have Melissa's current address, since you were still her legal guardian. So they called the agency and gave them the same song and dance and the upshot of all this cloak and dagger running around was that I got the name of the foster home, which was strictly against agency rules."

"That sounds like something out of a story book," I said incredulously.

"Doesn't it? But wait. That's just the beginning. Your Aunt Elfreda discovered Melissa was gone the same day I did, and she was furious." I could picture Aunt Elfreda. The maddest I ever saw her get was over the Jimmy business, which caused a few tight lines around her mouth. 'Furious' probably meant a stony silence and a look in her eye that would stop clocks.

"Did she call you?" I asked Don.

"No, I hopped right over to her house on the off chance that common sense had prevailed and the baby was there. She was ready to call the police, but I assured her *that* wouldn't do any good, so we put our heads together and decided to take matters into our own hands."

"What did you do?" I was beginning to enjoy this story.

"We decided to get Melissa. Just like that. I had once worked for a child welfare agency, so I knew their procedures only *look* tough. Really they are unbelievably full of holes. So I called up the foster mom and introduced myself as the agency supervisor. I and said there had been a mistake; that Melissa was supposed to be with Mrs. Boyle because we had a particularly interesting child that we wanted to place with this lady the next day. I said I was *so* sorry, but if she could have Melissa ready in an hour, I would be over to get her. Luckily I knew a little bit about Melissa's habits so I was able to ask if she was tolerating the new formula and if the rash on her face was better...that kind of thing..."

"Does she have a rash on her face?" That sounded worrisome.

"Not anymore, but she did then. It wasn't anything at all, but it made me sound like someone who had read her records. I was so convincing that by the time we showed up at the foster home, I was asking the foster mom for legal papers, not the other way around. I wanted to be sure I had the hospital release and the pediatrics report and all that stuff. She absolutely never questioned me. Your aunt was great. She was calm and acted slightly bored and asked all the right questions about eating and sleeping."

"Ooo...." I could imagine it. "I wish I had been there!"

"Me too." Don put a little kiss on his fingers and rubbed it onto my nose. "But when we got that baby into my car, your aunt really went wild. No baby in the world ever got so hugged and kissed and smiled at and talked to and rocked...poor thing, she finally got overwhelmed and started to cry, but by then we were blocks away and neither of us cared."

I was smiling and laughing just trying to picture it. Then I suddenly thought about Miss Page Boy Bob. "What happened when the agency found out?"

Don laughed. "You're not going to believe this. They didn't find out for nearly two weeks!"

"They didn't?" I couldn't imagine it.

"Nobody checked. This was an experienced foster mother, so if she didn't call with complaints or questions they figured she was getting along fine. And when the 'interesting child' never materialized she just figured something had gone wrong and plans had been changed again. Happens all the time."

"Don, why didn't either of you tell me?"

"We talked about it. But we figured if you thought Melissa was still in the hospital you wouldn't worry about her, and we were afraid we might end up in court, which would scare you unnecessarily."

"Unnecessarily? Why are you so cocky about court, whatever that means."

Don looked disgusted. "Because, my thick headed, suspicious friend, nobody could take Melissa away from you, and the best place to *prove* that would have been in court. How many times have I told you that?"

"So what happened?"

"Well you know, it's funny who your friends turn out to be. That nursery head nurse is going to have a special place in heaven as far as I'm concerned. Of course she knew your aunt—after all, your aunt had been up to see the baby every single day—and she knew me for the same reason. So when the agency worker suddenly appeared with all sorts of official looking papers, the nurse was very surprised and suspicious."

"Did she know about me?"

"Who? The nurse? Of course she knew about you. She was very, very sympathetic. A lovely gal. You think your aunt didn't talk about you all the time?"

"How would she help with this court thing?" I hadn't forgotten how this subject came up.

"When the agency finally *did* find out that Melissa was gone…they wanted to take her in for a doctor's exam I think…that know-it-all worker went storming over to the hospital to confer with good old Dr. Kildare, your friendly family physician."

"The OB?"

"Who else? And it took him about thirty seconds to connect me with the mystery."

"I don't understand."

"Remember, I had given him hell once about thinking he could get Melissa away from you. So he figured correctly that I did what I did. He got me on the phone and announced that unless I had Melissa back where she belonged, I would not only be out of a job, I would be in jail."

"What did you say to him?"

"I said I'd think it over and I hung up on him. I was betting that he would know enough not to call the police."

"Oh Don." My eyes must have been as wide as saucers. "You could have been in awful trouble couldn't you?"

Don raised his eyebrows speculatively. "You know, just about then that occurred to me."

"Then what?"

"I'm not sure. I think Dr. Awful and Miss Baby Snatcher retraced our steps. It must have seemed odd that I would know where to find Melissa. Somehow, anyway, they ended up in the newborn nursery grilling my friend, the head nurse."

"She didn't know anything, did she?"

"She'd seen the foster mom, and she knew that their records department had gotten her address. But the important thing was that she raised the question of how your OB had the authority to check Melissa out of the hospital. And when he started in on the unfit mother routine she got mad, bless her heart, and told him he was out of line and she would report it to the proper authorities. I guess they had a real shout-down—started all the babies crying and had half the hospital listening in. As soon as it was over, she phoned me and told me to get a lawyer *fast*."

"Did you?"

Don chuckled a little. "I really should have been a horse thief. How did a man with the instincts of a poker player ever end up in professional do-gooding?"

"I don't follow you."

"I called their bluff. Didn't get a lawyer. Didn't tell my department chief. Didn't do a damn thing."

From beyond the white curtain, I heard Ruthie explode. "You're kidding!"

Marcella let us hear her laughing as well.

"You sneaks! You've been listening," I said indignantly through the cloth barrier.

Ruthie said apologetically, "As Don gets more excited, his voice gets louder. Some horse thief!"

"Well come to think of it, I did call Elfreda right away." Don stood up and shoved the curtain back. He was talking to all three of us. "What a smooth operator she is! Didn't faze her. She said the social worker had phoned and wanted to come over and Elfreda said 'No, there was nothing to be accomplished by that,' and when the social worker asked about Melissa, Elfreda said she would have to discuss it with Melissa's mother, and hung up on her too. She said she doubted very much that she would hear from them again."

Don strolled over and sat up on our window-sill, holding a philodendron in his lap. "So, ladies, what do you think about all that?"

Ruth looked at me thoughtfully. "Betsy, why don't we arrange for you to see Melissa."

I was startled. Everything was coming at me at once.

"Could I?" I looked at Don. "Could I, Don?"

Don was admiring Ruthie. "You'll have to tell us how that's done. I only do kidnappings."

"I'll arrange it," she said confidently. "Just don't ask any questions." She grinned at me. "Betsy, I wouldn't believe I could feel this happy lying in this crummy bed. I swear sometimes there actually is justice in the world."

Marcella eased herself to a sitting position, slowly slid her feet to the stool by her bed, and carefully stood up and stepped down. She walked a few paces over to where Don was perched and put out her right hand. "Put'er there, pardner." Solemnly, they shook hands.

I looked at all three of them, grinning their heads off, and suddenly realized that my life was again spinning out of control. But for once I was willing to let someone else make the plans.

CHAPTER 8

▼

AUNT JANINE

True to her word, one day Aunt Janine came to see me. I heard a little tap on the door during afternoon visiting hours, and there she was, standing in the doorway, big and solid ("built like a tank," Joey once said) and unsmiling as usual. Sensible flowered cotton dress, plain black coat, grey hair pulled back into a knot, no lipstick. No wonder Tony was afraid of her.

"Well Betsy," she said firmly, as though she was about to tell me to open my arithmetic book. She walked to my bed and handed me a small plant. "I thought a plant made more sense than flowers. Last longer." She stood there and studied me. "You're looking well. I'd forgotten how pretty you are."

I motioned her to sit, and that seemed to confuse her. She looked around until she spied a straight chair at the end of Ruthie's bed. Self-consciously she went over, pulled that chair to the end of my bed and sat down. It was obvious that she didn't want to get too close to me. She clutched her big purse in her lap and waited for me to say something.

"Gee, Aunt Janine, it's great to see you," I said, hoping that didn't sound too much like I was criticizing her. "Thanks for coming."

"Joe tells me that you're doing very well. And I've enjoyed getting to know your friend Polly."

We sat in silence for a few minutes and neither of us could think of what to say next. Suddenly a big opening occurred to me.

"I'm not contagious anymore you know, and the new drugs mean that I will really be well soon."

"Well I certainly didn't mean to suggest that I'm afraid of you, Betsy. Yes, I had heard that they have fine medicine these days."

So then we talked about the drugs and when I might get out and about Joey. I asked Aunt Janine if she had seen Melissa and she said Joe took her over to Aunt Elfreda's and wasn't she a fine woman. And then that was pretty much that, until, with an awkward bustle, Aunt Janine gathered herself together, stood up, and said goodbye.

I really didn't expect to see her again. After all, she had done her duty, which was a big item with her. So you can imagine my surprise when there she was again during afternoon visiting hours, looking less uncomfortable but more determined than before. This time she sat in the arm chair next to my bed and started right in. It was obvious she had been thinking about something.

"Betsy, now that it looks as though you can put your illness behind you, I think it's time we had a talk."

I had no idea where she was going with this.

"I wondered if you would like to know more about your father."

My father had been Aunt Jenine's brother. I guess I seemed to agree because she plowed on.

"I had a long talk with Joe and Tony recently and they said I should talk to you. They said you all wondered why your father left your mother."

I said I assumed it was because my mother was alcoholic.

"That came later," Aunt Jenine explained. "He left because he was sick and he didn't want to be a burden."

"What was the matter with him?" I asked, though I had a hunch I could see what was coming.

"Joseph had tuberculosis, Betsy. That's where you caught it." When that didn't seem to upset me she went on. "They all had it."

"Pardon? Who all had it?"

"That's the story your brothers wanted you to hear. You know that my parents—your grandparents—came to this country from Cornwall in England in about 1890. Your grandfather was a miner and they settled in mining country in Michigan's Upper Peninsula. They had four children: Joseph, myself, Edward and Genevieve. We were very poor and lived on a small farm near Iron Mountain. We had no electricity or indoor plumbing of course, and not much medical care. Our parents kept a cow and raised chickens and vegetables, and when he could your grandfather worked in the mines.

"When he was about ten my brother Edward started to get sick—to do 'poorly' as my mother called it. He lost weight and had lots of colds and pretty soon was out of school most of the time. But in those days there wasn't a public health department, and we couldn't afford doctor's visits, and so we just assumed he had the grippe—that's a word you don't hear anymore—it means anything flu-ish. And then one day he just up and died. He was only a boy. But lots of families had children who died in those days. It was very sad but we were taught not to carry on about it because it was just one of those things.

"And then Gen got sick also. At that point our parents drove her in our horse and buggy to Marquette where there was a real hospital, and the doctors there decided she might have TB—they took some sort of specimen and found the germ. There weren't any TB hospitals yet, so she was sent home to be quarantined.

"For some reason our parents were asked to send a milk sample to the hospital to be tested. Sure enough—our cow had TB. That's where it was coming from. We didn't pasteurize our milk of course—it was just for us, we didn't sell it—you always assumed that your own cow was giving you good milk.

"I didn't know cows could get TB," I said.

"Neither did we. Gen didn't last very long—TB was called 'consumption' you know—the wasting disease—people just seemed to waste away. And it was very prevalent—lots of Upper Peninsula people died of it—and it was very shameful. You learned never, ever to talk about it."

"Why shameful? I've never understood that."

"Oh Betsy, it was like having leprosy. If it was known that TB was in someone's family, everyone avoided them because no one was sure how it spread—dirty people were thought to have it—it was a disease of poor people. Nice people pretended they didn't ever have it."

"But you didn't catch it?"

"I was the oldest—by the time we got Dot, our infected cow, I wasn't drinking any milk to speak of. I don't think my parents had it either, though we never knew for sure. And neither Edward and Gen had TB in their lungs—I suppose that's why nobody figured out what was wrong with Eddie."

I knew that TB could occur in the stomach and kidneys and blood and spine and all kinds of places in the body, so that didn't surprise me too much, but I wondered why my father didn't get sick sooner.

"My father was an adult," I observed.

"Yes, and that was the frightening thing about TB—you could have it for years and never be made sick, and then suddenly it would become active. Joseph assumed he was fine until right after Tony was born, and then suddenly he began to have the same symptoms that his sister had had. He knew right away what it was. But he was afraid if he told your mother the whole ugly secret would be out and the family would be disgraced. And of course he was afraid he might give it to you kids. So he decided just to leave. He did send your mother money from time to time—did she tell you that?"

"I don't remember. She always hinted that there was another woman, but I didn't believe that."

"Well we sort of lost track of Joseph. Our parents were old and not very well, and I guess he thought I was needed to take care of them so he never got me involved. He pretty much disappeared. I found out some years later that he ended up in a state sanitorium in New York State."

"Where he died?"

"Where he died."

"What about your parents?"

"I stayed on the farm with them until my father died, and then I brought my mother to live with us here. She died about ten years ago."

"And you're ok?"

"Yes. But I can't get over the feeling that TB isn't something one should talk about. I find it hard to say the word."

"You must have thought I was a terrible person, what with one thing and another. To run away, and get pregnant and all."

"Well I'll admit to some impatience. But I had my hands full with your brother Tony, and I'm a person who believes in worrying about one thing at a time. And not getting upset about something I can't do anything about. That's why I washed my hands of your mother. I will not let my life be complicated by someone who is her own worst enemy. And Betsy, I strongly advise you to do the same."

"Oh well, I don't think my mother wants anything to do with me, so that's not really a problem, is it?"

CHAPTER 9

▼

LOVE

One Sunday, Ruthie's husband, whose name was Elliott, came in pushing a wheelchair. Ruthie usually went downstairs to a friend's office to see her children on Sundays, so I figured that's what was going on. But this time, Elliott came over beside my bed and motioned me into the chair. I realized what was happening and started to give an excited little scream, but both Elliott and Ruth put forefingers to their lips to hush me.

"Once he gets you to the elevator, you're in business," Ruthie explained. "With Miss E. off duty, nobody else is going to pay attention."

My heart was beating really fast. This was more exciting than the time I walked out. At least that time I got myself prepared beforehand.

"Don is bringing your aunt and Melissa. They'll meet you downstairs," Ruthie said.

"How long can I stay?" I wasn't sure how long Ruthie stayed when she went.

"Bets, you're going to be confused and overwhelmed. Don't be hard on yourself if you have to leave fairly quickly. We can do this again soon."

"Oh no," I said. "I want to stay as long as I can."

And this time Ruth was wrong. When Elliott wheeled me into the small office waiting room, Aunt Elfreda was sitting in one of the plastic chairs holding a little pink bundle. Melissa was asleep, so I couldn't see her face, but I was startled at how small she was. She had on a pink bonnet and sweater and was wrapped up in a pink blanket. I just stared and stared and I couldn't think what to say. Elliott smiled at Aunt Elfreda and said, "I'll wait down the hall. Come and get me when she's ready to go back."

Aunt Elfreda stood up and said, "Well there now, Melissa, here's your mama." She walked over and started to hand Melissa to me.

I got scared. "I don't know what to do, Aunt Elfreda. She'll catch something. I won't know how to hold her."

But Aunt Elfreda acted like she hadn't heard me. She put this lumpy little package into my arms and untied her bonnet. "There, now, let's let Mama have a good look at your face." She pulled back the blanket. "Let's get this thing loosened up before you get too warm."

Then she reached into her big brown bag and pulled out a baby bottle of milk. "If she starts to cry, give her this," she said to me.

Then she left us alone together.

I gazed down at the tiny sleeping face in my arms. But she looks just like Polly Jo, I thought with amazement. Why didn't anyone tell me that? The little round cheeks and the hint of dimples and the fuzzy brown hair didn't look anything like me at all. Of course they also looked like Jimmy, only I didn't want to think about that.

"I should have called you Polly," I whispered and at that she opened her eyes and gazed back at me. She had blue eyes. She yawned and started to squirm. I tried moving her around on my arm but she arched her back and whimpered. I remembered holding Tony when he was a baby and I tried to think what to do. I unwrapped the blanket all the way and I held her against my shoulder and patted her. It was the wrong thing to do. She started to cry in my ear.

"There, there, Melissa," I said a little desperately. "Here, let's try this."

I propped her into a sort of sitting position and got out the bottle. I tried to stick it in her mouth, but she just yelled louder. I was nearly in tears myself when the door opened and Don poked his head in.

"Trouble?" he said hesitantly.

"Where's Aunt Elfreda?" I said tensely, trying to make the bottle stay in Melissa's mouth so she'd stop crying.

Don came all the way in. "Elliott took your aunt for some coffee. I said I'd stand watch."

He studied my situation. He took the handles of the wheelchair, unlocked the wheels and pushed me over to a green plastic settee.

"Let's try something," he said calmly over Melissa's howls. "Hand her to me."

He took Melissa from me and gently cradled her against his chest. The change of scenery quieted her for a minute.

"Why don't you sit on that couch," Don suggested.

I wasn't sure what he had in mind, but cautiously I slid from the wheelchair onto the setee.

"Put your arm on the arm rest," he said. He handed me the baby bottle with his free hand. Then he sat down beside me and put Melissa in the crook of my arm.

"I don't think she was getting any milk in the position you had her," he explained. "Just relax and tip the bottle way up so that all the milk is at the nipple end, like this."

He moved my hand and suddenly Melissa stopped squirming and started to suck at the bottle. I breathed a sigh of relief.

Don leaned back and put his arm across the top of the setee with his hand on my shoulder. He gave me a little squeeze. "Nobody said it was easy," he said with a smile.

"How do you know what to do?" I asked in astonishment.

"I told you I worked in child welfare once. I'm an old hand. Don't be discouraged."

I could feel myself choking up. "What if she doesn't like me?" I said.

Don put his arm down around my shoulders and tipped his head against mine. "Sweetie, she hasn't got any choice. You're her mother. You'll do fine."

I asked the awful question. "What if I turn out to be like my mother?"

Just then Melissa pushed out the bottle and whimpered. Without thinking, I put her on my shoulder again and patted her. She burped all over me and then was ready for the bottle again. Don got a clean diaper out of the brown bag, wiped my shoulder off, and then left the diaper there.

"Are you anything like your mother?" he asked gently.

I thought about it. Tony was like Mom—but Joey and I are like our dad, I thought. What a nice idea. I leaned my head on Don's shoulder and closed my eyes. I felt so peaceful.

"Why are you so nice to me?" I said sort of idly to Don. I didn't expect an answer.

"Because I love you, silly one. Don't you know that?" I felt his lips brush my face. It seemed like the most natural response in the world. I was afraid to open my eyes for fear things would change.

"Are you listening?" he whispered. "Shall I say more or am I way out of line?"

I felt the bottle go limp in my hand. I opened my eyes and looked at Melissa. She was asleep again. I rested the bottle on the table in front of me and then looked up at Don's bony, kind face. His gentle green eyes were looking at me cautiously, almost shyly. It was unlike him.

"You love everybody," I replied, not wanting to misunderstand.

"Not like this, I don't," he said, and kissed me softly on the lips. I put my free hand on his face and traced his nose and cheekbones with my fingers. I ran my fingertips across his sandy eyebrows and then rested my palm on his cheek. I didn't want to wake Melissa by moving very much.

"Am I just good old Don?" he asked hesitantly. "I can't tell. I shouldn't be doing this except I think you feel the same way about me."

I looked at Melissa and then I looked up at Don again. I had the vivid thought that I wished I could stay there forever.

"Is this what love feels like, do you suppose?" I said in wonderment.

"I don't know, is it? What do you feel?"

"If the world ended in the next hour I would feel perfectly happy."

Don laughed. "Gee, there's a romantic thought."

I was serious. "I mean, there's nothing more I could want in life than what I have this very minute."

"Really?" Don leaned over and kissed me again, harder and longer. It got to be really difficult not to move. I saw his point.

"Well...maybe not quite everything."

"Betsy, we're going to be together when you get out of this place aren't we? I'm not just flirting with you, sweetheart." He had tears in his eyes when he said that.

I realized I couldn't imagine life without him. While I hadn't even been noticing he had crept into the most central place in my heart and suddenly my heart was filled. I managed to say it to him just that way. I was awed by my certainty and by my calmness. Usually I was the person out of control and Don was the steady one. This time we switched places.

"Wow," Don said with his eyes wide. He wiped away his tears with the back of his hand. "Gee whiz. I had my cornflakes this morning just like an ordinary day, and before noon I'm engaged." He sat on the edge of the sofa and stared at me. "That did mean you would marry me, didn't it?"

I nodded. He flung both his arms wide and then clutched his head in frustration. Melissa slept on like nothing was happening. "Melissa," Don said to her. "You are intruding. Damnation. I suppose if you put her down somewhere she'd start to cry again and then we would have an audience for sure. Little girl..." he touched her short nose, "I am going to have to teach you appropriate behavior."

He laughed and tried to kiss me again, but instead slid off the couch and ended up on the floor. He put his arms around my legs and rested his face on my knees. I laid my hand on his hair and ruffled it.

Just then we heard a tap on the door, and Aunt Elfreda peeked in. When she saw us there she got all flustered and tried to say how sorry she was, but Don let go of me and stood up.

"Come in, come in Elfreda," he said briskly, marching over and pulling her into the room. "I'm glad you will be the first to know." He motioned her into the wheelchair. "Sit down first. Mrs. Boyle, would you object if your adopted niece and I decided to get married?"

Then Aunt Elfreda said the most surprising thing. "Betsy is already married," she said sternly.

I knew her well enough to know what she was thinking. "No, Aunt Elfreda, it isn't that way. Don has been a perfect gentleman. My goodness, you know that. Anyway, how can I be married to someone I haven't seen for six months?"

"Elfreda," Don said carefully. "I doubt that Betsy was ever legally married. I'll bet it can be annulled. But anyway, we're just making plans. Don't worry, this time everything will be done correctly. Aren't you going to be glad for us?"

He looked so remorseful and sad that even Aunt Elfreda's puritan heart was softened.

"Well," she said to him. "You're a very nice young man. And heaven knows Betsy has been through enough." She gave him a small, embarrassed smile. "I wish I were younger myself. I'd give her some competition."

Don stooped down and wrapped his arms around her. "Just think Elfreda. You'll be stuck with me as a son-in-law, sort of. That's a lot of Thanksgivings and Christmases."

And then Aunt Elfreda did something I had only seen her do once before. She began to weep. "Why am I doing this?" she moaned. "I'm really glad."

But Don just held her and his own tears came back and he said, "It's been a hard life, Elfreda. Let us give you a little happiness."

Years later I would think of that day as the turning point in my life. Don used to tell me that I had been lucky to have been young when I learned about hard luck and tough times. Joey and I compared notes on that one and I guess we agreed that maybe in our case the hard luck had been overdone. Anyway we always knew that nothing guaranteed you would get good times for a lifetime, but we knew what Don meant. We never took the good times for granted. Also we never planned ahead much. But I never froze up inside like Aunt Elfreda had done. Her bad times came too late and too fast I guess. She'd never learned to say to herself, "Oh that? That's just temporary. It'll pass."

CHAPTER 10

▼

HOME AT LAST

When Don first talked to Aunt Elfreda about moving into her house, she was disapproving. "People will talk." Don didn't smile at that, he just pointed out seriously that she always had roomers and people didn't talk about them.

"That's different," she protested.

"How's it different?"

Then she got all flustered and it took a little while for Don to get across the idea that it would be good for Melissa to have him there so she could begin to know him as a parent. Aunt Elfreda couldn't very well argue with that. So about two weeks after we got engaged, Don moved his things into my old room. Aunt Elfreda wouldn't ever rent it out, of course, and she kept the baby in with her, so Melissa wasn't using it either.

Don was impatient to get married. We thought maybe the hospital people would let me have a few days in a private room and we'd get married in the chapel like Polly Jo and Joey had recently done. But at a big case conference—we heard later that there was a lot of bad feeling—it was decided that I wasn't to be allowed to "shortcut the cure this time," as they put it. It seemed like their way of getting even with me, frankly. I knew that sanatorium patients got regular weekend furloughs and I never heard that it hurt them; but "time will tell" was always the answer we got when we talked about what san patients were allowed to do.

Don got right to work on my annulment and he turned out to be right. My marriage "had never been consummated," as they worded it at the court house. Jimmy never challenged us, so I was free in a very short time.

Ruth and Elliott were really indignant when the hospital staff said I couldn't get married till I was discharged—it looked as if that would be another six months or so—and Ruthie went into a huddle with some of her medical pals.

"Leave it to us," she told me confidently. "We'll think of something."

Don would sit by her bed by the hour where I couldn't hear what they said. "Tell me!" I would beg, but they wanted it to be a big surprise and wouldn't tell me a thing. Don's grins gave away that they were working things out though, and I began to feel like a kid waiting for Christmas.

So one Sunday, when Elliott got me to go down to see Melissa, I was taken instead to an examining room on the first floor. Polly Jo was waiting for me with a box in her arms and when Elliott left us alone she opened it. Inside was a beautiful blue silk robe and a pair of matching blue slippers. "We were afraid a dress would be too conspicuous, honey, but you'll will look darlin' in this robe." I stood up to put it on and then I looked at myself in the long examining room mirror. Polly Jo combed my hair. I looked fine.

"Am I getting married?" I asked her with a little gasp of excitement.

"You are unless you back out right now."

She handed me a clipboard with some legal papers on it. "Here," she said. "Sign this. We got a special dispensation for the marriage license."

After I sat back in the wheelchair I signed my name next to Don's. Then Polly Jo opened the door and pushed my wheelchair out into the hall. Joey was standing there holding a small white box. "Here," he said. It was an orchid. "From Don." Polly Jo pinned it on my robe, and the two of them pushed me down the hall toward the chapel.

As they opened the chapel door, I saw the back of people's heads and I recognized the Williams and Aunt Elfreda and Aunt Janine. Someone started to play the organ and Don appeared way down in front, standing beside Elliott. I saw Ruthie in a wheelchair in the front row and Marcella sitting in a pew. Everyone twisted around and looked at me. Polly Jo walked slowly in ahead of us, and Joey pushed my wheelchair up the aisle. The hospital chaplain, Reverend Edwards, appeared in front of us and then everything disappeared into a blur of tears.

Don saw what was happening and pulled a big clean hankie out of his pocket. "Just a minute" he said to the Reverend, and he bent over and wiped my eyes. "Here," he said as he handed me the hankie. Then he kissed me and whispered, "This won't take long. You can stand anything for five minutes," and grinned at the audience. I heard some sniffling out there so I guess I wasn't the only one who was crying.

It didn't take long, but I'll always remember that when Reverend Edwards said, "I pronounce you man and wife," he had to stop for a minute and clear his throat before he could say "let us pray." After he was done, he was the next person after Don to kiss me. You have to remember that I was still considered to be contagious (even though I wasn't and everyone should have known it) so I'll always remember what a sweet, kind thing that was for him to do.

Don explained later that they didn't dare try for a reception. The wedding was daring enough—the Reverend put his job on the line and so did a bunch of other people—and then they pulled off the biggest deal in the world; Don and I had a private room right there in the hospital. Just for one day and night.

The Internal Medicine Chief of Staff, Dr. Janowski, came through for me. In spite of the TB group's decision that I couldn't get married, he was the big boss, so he ordered up this room and (I heard later) paid for it himself. The only thing that went into my chart was a little note that I was in a single room "for mental health" and a suggestion that there were "psychiatric notes" somewhere. Dr. Janowski was a somber man with black eyebrows and nobody fooled around with him, so whatever the TB staff thought they kept quiet. Don claimed there were surprisingly few rumors. He said people loved us both and knew it had to be a real secret.

Somebody had hung a "contagious" sign on the door to the private room and also "Do not disturb." Before we went there, Don put on his white coat, so he looked like a doctor, and when he pushed me past the nursing station on the private floor the weekend charge nurse looked up briefly and winked at him. "Greatest woman in the world," he said to me.

Somebody had left a huge bouquet of flowers, a bottle of champagne and a big basket of food on the bureau. Compared to our wards upstairs, it seemed like a hotel room, with flowered curtains and a private bathroom. Don kidded me about no bedpans tonight, but he also suggested slyly that maybe I'd like him to help me take a shower for the first time in five months.

So that's how it started, after a wonderful hot shower (we'd both had several glasses of champagne by then)—in a private hospital room, with a bed so high and narrow we'd both have needed real medical attention if we'd lost control and fallen out, which we almost did.

When it started to get dark there was a little knock. Don put on a hospital gown and cracked open the door. It was the charge nurse with two dinner trays. Each one had a rose on it! "You'll have to get her back to her room before the day shift comes on," she warned him. He nodded and wheeled in our trays. We would have a whole night together! It seemed too good to be true.

CHAPTER 11

▼

TOUGH LUCK AND COMMON SENSE

They kept me in the hospital for five more months, even though the drugs supposedly were causing my disease to be arrested. Don was tempted to raise the devil about that, but he had Melissa to think about and he was afraid I would get too tired if I was home with her. No one understood that TB patients really were cured—somehow the word "cure" was never used in association with TB. We had gotten so used to thinking of TB as "arrested" that we were super cautious about everything. And truthfully, I think maybe the big shots thought a little punishment was not a bad idea for impulsive Betsy. Who knew what she was likely to do next.

Anyway, I did eventually go home to Aunt Elfreda's. And do you know what she did the day I came home? What a great lady she was. She took Melissa, who was just beginning to talk and crawl, to visit the Williams for a long weekend.

"You need a honeymoon my dear," she said to me.

So for four days Don and I were alone together. Even though I was frantic to have time with Melissa, Aunt Elfreda and Don were right about one thing. Too much excitement was not going to be good for me.

And I was unexpectedly uneasy with Melissa when she finally came back. It was like that time in the examining room, only multiplied by about a hundred. She didn't know me, and she didn't like it when I picked her up, and I was so stiff and scared that I scared her too. I found myself giving her to Aunt Elfreda or to Don so I wouldn't have to listen to her cry.

Finally one day Don said to me, "See here, Mom, the time has come for you to be in charge. After all, in the real world you would have had to muddle through by yourself some of the time. So after I go to work this morning, Aunt Elfreda is going to visit a friend for the day, and you and Melissa are going to get acquainted."

He reminded me that babies do cry, and it doesn't seem to hurt them, so if necessary I should let Melissa cry it out. "She's a smart little girl and she's a bit spoiled, so don't let her bully you."

I won't pretend that that day didn't last forever—I kept looking at the clock—but I discovered that if I just went about my business Melissa's whimpering would eventually stop and she would find something to do. So then after that I felt more like a real mom, not just a practice one.

And throwing away common sense, within a year I was pregnant again. When Don said no to the idea of another baby, I just ignored him, and because those were the early days of the Pill, how did he know whether I was taking them or not. I guess he was glad—he knew I needed to make up for losing Melissa the way I did—but we had some tense months wondering if everything would be okay. But Donnie came bursting into the world with a smile on his face. Well maybe not quite that, but he turned out to be a happy baby, a real charmer just like his dad.

And when that worked out so well, three years later we had a baby girl. By then I began to wonder if maybe I'd overdone it, but I took Aunt Janine's advice and didn't worry about more than one thing at a time, and that seemed to help.

*   *   *   *

Five years went by and I was gradually learning how to be a real person. One hot day in June Polly Jo and I were sitting in plastic recliners under my oak tree, watching our kids play. Jodie, her little girl, was three and so was our Donnie. My new baby, another girl, named for Aunt Elfreda's Judy, was sleeping inside. Melissa was six by then and was her Aunt P.J.'s best pal in the world. What a pair!

Our husbands were at work; Don was the social service administrator at the hospital now and complained all the time about how he hated it. "All rules, no patients...what am I doing in this terrible job?" he would moan. But I heard from Ruthie and others that he had shaken up the whole service and was admired by lots of people all over the hospital.

Joey had found a job in the city and was still working nights because he had gone back to school, studying some kind of engineering technology. Polly Jo didn't see much of him, but she never complained. She knew that when he was earning more money she could go back to school herself, maybe even go back to nursing school, and they were looking ahead.

Aunt Elfreda had quit taking boarders and instead spoiled us rotten by being our live-in baby sitter. I could never have managed three little kids without her. But we tried to spoil her too, and sometimes I would see her smiling to herself as if she couldn't quite believe it.

Polly Jo and I were planning a reunion. Ruthie wanted to have it at her big house but we said no, we wanted it at Aunt Elfreda's. Ruth had to be more careful than we did because she never had taken any of the anti-TB drugs. I felt sorry for her. I could remember what it was like to have that time bomb ticking away in your lungs. She was thinking of becoming a radiologist—someone who read X-rays—because it was easy and the hours were regular.

Marcella was coming back to town for a few days and we all wanted to see her. She'd had a hard time; she'd been sick for so long that her family had mostly drifted away, and she wasn't very strong even though she looked big and tough. She worked as a restaurant cashier and I think she just barely got by. We hated to ask very many questions because we felt so lucky compared to her.

We wanted to invite a few others from the hospital days; Charlie, Rachel, our dietician, even Professor Adams, who Joey got acquainted with at his school—the professor recognized our last name.

Polly Jo pushed her folding chaise back into a reclining position and looked up into the trees.

"What about Dave?" she asked musingly, sort of half kidding.

"I don't care what happened," I said. "I'd like to see him. You're the one who might feel funny. Anyway, he probably wouldn't come."

Polly Jo glanced over at me. "I'm not so sure." She laughed. "He's probably told himself that he broke my heart and he owes it to me to make me feel better."

"Maybe he'll try to start something again."

"Oh no, that's not how it works. He thinks these things just happen. Poor Dave is the victim of fate, don't you know that?"

"How are things with his wife, do you know?"

"Rachel tells me he's had at least two girl friends since me." Polly Jo sighed. "I think he's crazy. Maybe his wife manages not to know."

"You didn't think he was crazy when it was you."

She scowled at me. "I was the crazy one. You used to tell me that all the time. I was just lucky that Joe came along when he did."

"Luck is a funny thing, isn't it?"

"Don't be sarcastic…"

"I'm not being sarcastic. Think how lucky we were to find Joey and Don."

"And to know Jimmy and Dave, and to have TB, and to have dim-witted mothers."

"Polly Jo! Your mother isn't dim-witted. What are you talking about?"

"My mother only sees what she wants to see. Did you know that Jimmy wrote to her for money?"

Now it was my turn to sigh. In the back of my mind was a nagging thought that Jimmy would come back and Melissa would like him. We had to tell her about him, of course, because the Williams were her grandparents and we wanted her to know that. But of course she called Don "Daddy" and he <u>was</u> her daddy legally. Still…

"Your mom sent him money?"

"Of course. Nothing is too much for our Jimmy."

"Do you suppose he'll ever come back?"

"And face you and Melissa? I doubt it. He wants Mom and Dad to come to California."

"Maybe that would be good for them."

"You're kidding."

We sat without talking for a few minutes. It was a hot summer day and the shade felt good. The kids wanted to turn on the hose and I said they could. They came and dribbled water on our legs. It startled us both awake.

"Do you ever think that the time in the hospital was a good thing for you?" I asked Polly Jo.

"Well, I've wondered what I'd be doing if it hadn't happened. Probably nursing somewhere and running around with the doctors the way Rachel does."

"Not married?"

"Who knows. But not to Joey, and that would be too bad. We're good for each other. I meant it when I said that was luck."

"For him too."

"Right." She thought for a minute. "What would you be doing if you hadn't gotten sick?"

"Oh I think about that a lot. Probably Joey would have escaped and I'd have been trapped with our mother. I'd probably still be there."

"So it was lucky for you too."

"It sure didn't seem like it at the time."

"You never know."

"Right."

We were quiet again.

"Polly Jo?"

"What?" she said lazily.

"Does anything scare you?"

"Not much. You?"

"Not very much. That's funny isn't it? Aunt Elfreda's the same way. I'm glad of that, aren't you?"

"Never thought about it. I suppose so."

"It's like I was so scared for so long I ran out of fear."

"Yeah."

I thought about that some more. It was true.

"Bonesy?"

"What?"

"Let's don't invite Dave. No point in tempting fate."

"Okay."

"Good. There's such a thing as pressing your luck, I guess."

"Right. Let's don't press our luck." I smiled at Polly Jo. We talked brave, but we both knew that good times could disappear with the sunshine, and we both knew that luck and bravery were hitched up with common sense. We didn't take anything for granted.

We didn't invite Dave.

CHAPTER 12

▼

EPILOGUE

One day in 1988 my granddaughter Lissa unexpectedly appeared at my door in the late afternoon. Because the old house—I still lived in the house Aunt Elfreda left me—was a fair distance from Lissa's house, and because she is only ten years old, I rarely saw her by herself. So this was a special treat. But I wondered how she got there, to the wrong side of town, all alone.

"I rode the bus," she told me a little belligerently. "I know how to ride the bus, Gramma Bee."

Did her mother know she was here?

"I called her from school. At work. She said it was okay."

And what was the occasion for this unexpected visit? "Umm," she said, and then she hesitated. "I'm supposed to interview you."

Gosh. I was certainly honored but I wondered why.

"You've had an interesting life," she said, a little embarrassed. I had the feeling that wasn't the whole story.

So I invited her in, found her a coke in the frig, and we sat down at the same kitchen table where so many years ago Aunt Elfreda and I had formalized our informal arrangement. Lissa is small like her mom, with curly brown hair and that unmistakable Williams face. I'm not sure how much she knows about that side of her heritage. Both her Williams great-grandparents have been dead for years and as far as I knew she thought of my husband as her grandpa.

But evidently not.

"Gramma," she said. "A man came to the house yesterday when Mom was at work, and when I answered the door…"

I interrupted her. "You don't answer the door when it is someone you don't know."

"But he knew my name."

"Okay," I said hesitantly, reminding myself that she seemed to be all right. "And?"

"He was an old guy, maybe older even than you."

"Gee thanks."

"You know what I mean. He was really old. He looked like he was maybe homeless—had a white beard and sort of shabby clothes. You know."

"What did he want? How did he know your name?"

"He said he was my grandfather."

Oh my. Jimmy. My heart jumped but I controlled my expression and asked calmly, "And what did you do? I hope you didn't let him in."

"I was scared. I just said Sorry and shut the door. Then I locked it and called my mom. She seemed really upset and said she'd be right home, but under no circumstances to let him in, and to call next door and ask Mrs. Warnmont to come over."

"Did you?"

"Yes, but by the time she came he'd already left so I wasn't scared anymore."

"What did your mother tell you?"

"She said it might be true and I should come here and ask you about it."

"I'm surprised you didn't come last night. Or that your mother didn't let me know."

"She said she wasn't supposed to talk about it. She said it was up to you to tell me what you wanted me to know."

"So this isn't exactly a school assignment."

"No, but you really are the most interesting person I know. And if he really is my grandfather then I'd like to hear the story. I can take it, Gramma. I know about stuff. You don't have to be afraid to tell me."

I was impressed by the persistence of this junior detective; she reminded me very much of her great-aunt PJ and I suspected there was no point in trying to put her off. But this meant I had to think about some things that I didn't like to think about. Things that were still painful so that I pushed the memories down even when they surfaced in dreams. And yet, what did I owe to this earnest, grownup little ten year old? What should I tell her about Jimmy? And what on earth was he doing here, and what on earth did he want from Lissa and her mom after all these years?

"I'll tell you what," I said to her. "Yes, that may have been your grandfather. Your biological grandfather. But let's remember that Grampa was the grandfather that counts. He's the guy who played with you and taught you to ride a bike and told you stories. You tell your mom I said that and she can explain what I mean. Its a very long story. Suppose you and your mother come over tomorrow for supper and I'll answer your questions. Okay?"

After Lissa left I found myself remembering. I remembered that when I originally escaped from the hospital when I was eighteen, I really had believed that somehow I would live happily ever after. It seemed as though I had used up a lifetime of bravery and God had better not test me again. Even when I let myself understand that things could still go wrong, I never believed that the worst would happen. I knew other people who had had a series of terrible events happen to them, Marcella for instance, but that was her, and of course I privately believed I was different. I know now that everyone thinks that—it's how we keep ourselves from being scared all the time. But when the very, very worst really did happen, there was a little corner of my mind that kept waiting for it to go away—that believed it couldn't be happening to me.

Melissa and Lissa came to dinner the next night after Jimmy's surprise visit. Melissa brought her famous slum gulleon—beef, tomatoes and noodles in a casserole. I had thrown together an apple pie in memory of Aunt Elfreda, for whom such family events were central. Usually Aunt Elfreda's old oak dining-room table would be covered with food and my three kids and their spouses, plus my five grandchildren would be here too. But tonight I wanted just to tell the Jimmy story to Melissa and Lissa. After all, Don had been the real father of my other children. Everyone else who was important to the story was dead. Talk about irony. Here I was, half way through my sixties, with my bad lungs and melodramatic history, and all the rest had quietly slipped away.

Polly Jo should be here, I thought sadly—but Polly Jo's luck had run out twenty years ago. Instead of living happily ever after, she developed breast cancer. After she died Joey took their two kids as far away as he could go—far from me, far from his past, to be where he could forget and start over. He bought property in Nebraska and learned cattle ranching—how's that for a city boy who'd never been interested in the outdoors? I guess he was like Teddy Roosevelt—he thought if he and the kids worked hard outdoors they would be so strong they wouldn't ever get sick. So far, so good. I visited him once, but I need more company than that. His nearest neighbor lived over the horizon. After his kids were grown he got married again to a tough minded Nebraska widow who takes good care of him.

Don and I went through some really rocky years. I won't tell Lissa about that. He married me when I was still a kid, but I didn't stay a kid forever, and I got tired of being bossed around by somebody who thought he was my father. We separated twice. Finally I calmed down and didn't always insist on having my own way. Don calmed down too and didn't try to always explain everything to me. The big thing was that eventually I actually believed that my TB was cured. Then I started to live flat out. I got a GED and then went to our community college and learned accounting—that took some getting used to by Don, but he did have a kind heart, and he was glad when I didn't have to be an invalid anymore. As soon as all three kids were safely in school I got a job in the front office at the college, which was fun.

Don lived into his seventies and died suddenly of a heart attack just a few years ago. No warning, no years as an invalid, his reward, I have always said, for putting up with so much from me. So now I'm alone, except that Melissa and the others still live nearby, so I haven't anything to complain about.

But this Jimmy business caught me by surprise. How could such a spoiled skunk have lived so long. Getting what he deserved, apparently, judging from Lissa's description. After I had told Lissa and her mother the whole story, Melissa asked me if I planned to see him. I found that to be an awful idea. "Not if I can help it," I told Melissa. "No doubt he wants money."

What I forgot was that Jimmy would know where I lived. Or he guessed. But being forewarned I had a time to collect my thoughts before I answered the doorbell the next day. There he was—Mickey Rooney. I couldn't help it—the resemblance made me laugh.

"Betsy?" He wasn't sure. I'm not skinny anymore, of course, and I have fly-away pepper and salt hair and brown skin with lots of wrinkles from too many afternoons in the garden. I'm a long way from that pale, thin Joan Fontaine of yesteryear.

"Hello Jimmy," I said. "Please come in." I had decided the best approach was to be formal and firm. We walked into the livingroom and sat across from each other in the old tan overstuffed chairs. "Why are you here?"

Jimmy tried a little levity. "Just wanted to see the old gang," he said cheerily. "Wanted to see how the kid turned out."

"Uh huh." I certainly didn't have a reply to that nonsense.

Silence. "You're okay I see." he persisted. "Too stubborn to let a little TB get you down. You got plenty of money, I gather."

And there it was. I could have asked him how he was getting along, but my late Aunt Janine lived on in me and I summoned up my memory of her. I said, "I don't think we have anything to talk about, Jimmy. Please leave us all alone."

He stood up because I did—I think he'd have sat there all morning otherwise—and started to string out a long pathetic spiel about his hard luck, but I just kept walking toward the front door. When I opened it, I said "goodbye," and then "goodbye" again when he tried to go on talking, and then "goodbye" again as I slowly closed it on him. Finally he made an obscene gesture, turned and headed down the walk.

And with Jimmy's departure I had a funny sense that the last chapter of my long ago past had finally closed. After more than half a century I was finally, completely, inexorably, irreversibly cured.

978-0-595-37890-6
0-595-37890-0

Printed in the United States
51696LVS00005B/397-498